A FAR VOICE CALLING

A FAR VOICE CALLING

Margaret Weeks Adair

DOUBLEDAY & COMPANY, INC.

GARDEN CITY, NEW YORK

Jacket and endsheet drawings by Lillian Obligado

Library of Congress Catalog Card Number 64-16236
Copyright © 1964 by Margaret Weeks Adair
All Rights Reserved
Printed in the United States of America

TO
MORRIS
AND WIS AND ROD

BEFORE YOU BEGIN:

You should know that the far voice may have been only the sound of the river or the sea. It could of course have been Toivo's ambition calling him, or a whisper to Hadge from his homeland.

Perhaps it was the voice of human conscience that spoke to Aarni of a brotherhood of men.

Or was it a voice from a time of companionship long gone but strangely echoing in the memory of an intelligent sea creature?

It may have been all of these, a far call to each man and beast that he alone could hear—or only the sound of the river or the sea.

M.W.A.

A FAR VOICE CALLING

ONE

Smoothly, breaking scarcely a ripple on the surface of the great river over which he skimmed his light craft, Toivo Jarvenin slid his oars in and out of the water. Except for the creaking cry of an occasional late gull or the tiny splash of a leaping salmon, only the rhythmic friction of rowlocks made any sound to disturb that July evening.

This silence of the river at full flood, as its wild rush halted and it hesitated to merge with the sea, a more adult traveler might have thought to compare to a caught breath or to a stayed moment in time. To Toivo, the shock-haired boy in the skiff, whose sea blue eyes today held none of the peace around him, it was simply "quiet water—no wind." And he guessed he'd best make headway while the going was good.

To his right now as he rowed up the Columbia toward the shadowed cove and weathered houseboat that he called home, the lights of the cannery's fish scow were far away and dim in the mist, closer to the Washington side at this point in mid-channel than to the Oregon shore. The tide was high, and that was good; for water would be deep over the mud flats and he could tie up at the door of the house when he got there, instead of making fast at the lower float and lugging his gear up the ladder. There'd be time then to get his fish cleaned for supper. Supper. His empty stomach squirmed at the thought of it, for he'd not eaten all day.

Keep your mind on the rowing, friend, he told himself. There's a good two miles yet to go.

It had been morning when Toivo began this trip out to the fish scow. He'd started as soon as the mail came in at the Svenson post office; for though his father, Hadge Jarvenin, had warned him many times that the channel of the Columbia was no place for a boy in a skiff even on the mildest of days, he knew that this letter from Hadge's brother in Finland, from the little town of Hameenlinna where the two men were born, would be welcome to the big fisherman who had stopped smiling.

It's always worth the trouble, anyway, to row out there, Toivo told himself. The trip put adventure into days that often stretched long otherwise, now that the district school was out, unless of course he was invited to the Rekkonens or Mr. Rekkonen brought his kids down river and left them for the day with Mrs. Ek, his sister and Toivo's good neighbor.

The Rekkonen kids. Toivo thought of them always with a grin and a feeling of affection. They too were "river kids," though they did not live in a houseboat as Toivo did. Their father fished the river and worked in the cannery, but they owned a piece of land and worked it. Aarni, larger of the two big Rekkonen boys, was a little older than Toivo and his best friend.

Crazy old Aarni, he thought now. And Olli—and Sis.

12

This trip today had given him things to tell them that would make those round blue eyes of theirs bug out a little more than usual; for they had never watched the seining horses.

He was to look back that night, remember this thought, and tell himself that he hadn't known the half of it; but that was later. Now his mind was busy going back over the events of the morning's trip.

I don't know if the excitement out there in the channel is just old stuff to Father, he was thinking, or if he's too plain stubborn to let himself enjoy it. But the way he acted this morning—wow!

For a moment the boy rested, feathered his oars, breathed deeply of the salt, cool air. Part of his thoughts still considered his father's behavior, but one corner of his mind admired the sunset and another corner noted a small breeze creeping in, riffling the water.

Hadge Jarvenin had indeed acted strangely. At first he had seemed all right. His large head, with its roughly cut hair topped by the pointed reindeer-hide cap from Lapland that he always wore, rain or shine, had lifted at sight of his son and the letter he was bringing. His face had brightened; but almost at once he was frowning again at some arriving gill netters and their fish catch; and without taking time to glance at his mail had shoved it into his pocket and gone doggedly back to work, weighing fish.

"Under thirty pounds, six cents a pound," he'd kept saying over and over again, making entries in the fishermen's credit books. "This, over thirty pounds, seven cents a pound. This one, steelhead, four cents." The fact that he hated the work was in his voice and written all over him. Thinking about this, Toivo picked up his oars and rowed on.

He hurries the men too much, thought the boy. They don't like it. And that hadn't been all.

When the steamer *T. J. Potter* came tooting around the bend, bringing vacationers from Portland, gay in bright colors and full of fun, Hadge had shrugged impatiently and refused even to glance her way; and when the tide began to run in over the sandspit and the seiners out there had to hurry their big horses and quickly add other horses to help draw up the bulging nets of salmon, then again hurry the horses onto scows that would serve as floating stables until the tide drained outward, the entire operation had taken place behind Hadge's wide back. He would not waste one look at a sight that other people often came far to see.

"Make room for those seiners," he had begun to order instead, as he urged the gill netters along. "You are not all. I have now the seiners' catch to weigh!"

Actually the men had not hurried much, but had done as they liked to do; they had talked. Always when they had lowered sails and tied up to come aboard the scow after long hours of lonely work they liked to trade news of their catch, of one another's families, or of anything else that interested them.

"Another harbor seal in the nets last night," some of them had reported while Toivo was there, pushing their sou'westers back from their faces, stamping their feet and swinging their arms to start the blood circulating, and shouting at the top of their voices because it was good to be heard when a man had a thing to tell. "The spotted kind. You know? Second one this week."

"Yeah," they said, and the word was a growl. "Plenty rough on the salmon catch, those devils!" A single blow on top of the head, that was the way to kill them.

"Spotted kind or any kind"—the fishermen nodded—"bad." Only one man had disagreed. He was younger than the others, red-haired, with a city haircut.

"Aw come on, listen!" this man had said. "Scientists claim this isn't true! They say that when they cut open dead seals they find hardly any salmon in their bellies at all, but that they're full of sculpin and squid, scrap fish —even small sharks. They say that instead of living on salmon, seals more than likely live mostly on the stuff that would harm salmon." He looked around at all the weathered faces scowling at him. "That's right! I read about it."

"*Ei!*" scoffed the other men; and they pulled down their mouths and made don't-tell-us-that motions with their hands, at the one who read such stuff. A fellow down near Astoria this morning, they went on to say to one another, had got something special. He'd shot one of the big tan seals, not so common as the spotted ones. "Those things have ears. And whiskers, by gar, like a dog."

"Big eyes too," the red-haired man had mumbled. "Eyes—like a dog's."

Hadge had seemed not to listen. He didn't listen to anything; and Toivo had not been able to hear any greetings or see any smiles or an exchange of any kind between his father and the other men. He'd been thinking about it all afternoon as alternately he drifted or fished or rowed in the sun on Cathlamet Bay. He was thinking of it now as he skimmed toward home in the last faint light of evening.

Father hasn't always been like this, he told himself; and recalled the years before his mother died, when the three of them had lived together in the clean, good-smelling house on Walluski Creek. In those years when Hadge Jarvenin, fresh from Finland with his training as an artist and his skill as a potter, still believed he could make a place for himself and his family in the American world of arts and crafts, he had been a laughing man— a huge clown of a man, to be sure, but sensitive to life and to the needs of people.

He misses those old days, thought Toivo. Both of us do. He's pretty bitter too, because his ability is not noticed here, while in his country all his family, from way back, rated a lot of respect for their skills. I know those are some of the reasons he's so unfriendly. And I'll bet the main reason he hates his job so much is the smell of that fish box. They say that sometimes when the waves roll high out there, the old scow bucks like a wild cayuse. That, with the fish smell— No wonder he comes home a lot of the time looking sort of green in the face, and mad at everybody. Frowning at the sky, estimating the length of remaining daylight, the boy sighed.

Offers to help him with his English don't do any good, either. He wouldn't give up his way of talking—any more than he'd give up that old-country cap!

Breathing hard, because he had come a long way and was very tired, Toivo again rested on his oars. The sun was almost down, shore line purpling, water silver-gray as cottonwood leaves and getting choppy.

Mr. and Mrs. Ek hadn't noticed that he wasn't home

16

yet, he supposed. Well, maybe they had. They often did call to him or come across the runway from their land to the houseboat to make sure he was all right; and they were his safeguards, when Hadge was away, against creeping loneliness.

It would be tougher navigating this last bit. Best get going. Bending for the stroke, he dipped his oars to pull and thought he heard a sound, off his bow; but when he turned his head to listen and completed the swing of the oars nothing was there.

What sort of sound had that been? he asked himself, looking uneasily into the oncoming darkness. Sort of a choking sound? Or a call? Had it been meant for him? Strong inside him was the conviction that it had indeed been for him and that he must find where it came from. And though his own common sense and his father's orders always to be off the river before dark were against it he began a crisscross search of the area.

For a long time he hunted, peering into shadows, moving slowly, for he could not leave without knowing the answer to this mystery, but he found nothing and heard nothing further. After a while when darkness made it impossible to see more than a few feet ahead of him he gave up.

Old river's fighting us, he thought, and unconsciously whispered the next words: "There's no use, whoever you are—if you are anyone." Haunted still by the lonely cry, but with fatigue and hunger claiming him, he bent once more to the rowing.

Head turned over shoulder now, he strained for a sight of a familiar landmark to tell him where he was. Sometime back he knew, he had passed the mouth of the Little John Day, and then a certain house. Now, easily discernible because of the white blaze down its length, he saw the black tree stump on the point; and his stroke steadied, became light, as it had been earlier in the day. The old stump meant that he was nearing the cove, that lamplight from the Eks' window would be showing any minute now. Steadily he stroked—then stopped, startled.

His oar had bumped something—a soft body. And he heard again that sound—like a choking call—like a sigh. Horrified, he peered down. He was looking into the whiskered, half-submerged face—the beseeching eyes of a baby seal. Half upright, leaning backward, the stricken little animal was making a weak effort to keep afloat, but losing its battle. Just why it was in so much trouble Toivo could not tell; but he had no doubt that it was asking him for help. Crazily, without thought, he shipped oars and dropped to his knees, reaching his arms to it; then drew back. That wasn't the way!

"What in blazes can I do?" he groaned, heart pounding and hands fumbling; and sent a wild and hopeful glance across the water. Useless. No one was coming to help him. No one even knew he was out here. He was in this alone.

"Can't just haul you in over the side," he said to the little seal. "Even somebody bigger than I am would swamp the boat that way." The skiff already was rocking broadside and shipping water. He steadied it. "Bet you've got teeth too, mister." The big eyes in the whiskered face looked back at him. Now they were full of panic, low in the water.

Toivo was a good swimmer, as were all the boys on

the river; but he knew that if this young animal, which must weigh somewhere around thirty pounds, should grab him in a drowning hold out there in the rough water there would be no chance of his saving either one of them.

He heard the sigh again, saw the baby seal make a convulsive struggle, then become still. The little animal had given up. It was sinking!

Almost before he knew it Toivo went into action. He kicked off his shoes. Two quick motions rid him of his shirt, his pants; another put him over the side of the skiff.

"Wow! Cold!" His body was shocked but refreshed; and swiftly, hand over hand, he worked along the gunwale to the boat's stern. Visibility here, low in the water, was better than he had thought it would be; but he must take care to move steadily, he told himself. Don't rush; don't turn the boat too much or it would bump the seal and send it to the bottom of the river. Best keep a hold with one hand on the boat too, until he saw if Mr. Whiskers was going to use his teeth.

He came around the stern, saw that the little seal was still afloat, was within his reach.

"Easy," he whispered, reaching out a hand, "easy now." His arm went about the small cylindrical body. "Come on, boy." There was no response. He thought perhaps the eyes had moved a little, but the baby seal seemed to have no strength as he drew it toward him. He held its head out of water, and it lay against his shoulder, its blunt nose near his neck. Then suddenly it was pressing against him, making nuzzling sounds.

"Hey!" Toivo jerked back. "Look, Joe, I'm *not* your

mamma!" Joe wouldn't believe that. He'd found warmth when he was chilled and strength when he was weak. Food, Joe seemed to be thinking, should be included in the deal! He was determined about this, and it made him hard to hold. Toivo hoped that he could get him quickly into the boat.

He tried pushing him over and in—with one hand, first, while with the other hand he clung to the skiff as it bounced and turned; then, letting go his hold on the gunwale, holding the seal with both hands, and treading water to keep his own face above the surface, he made an effort, as the skiff rolled low, to boost the little animal aboard.

It wouldn't be too much of a trick usually, the now-breathless boy began to tell himself. It's only that every time I manage to get a hold on this slippery seal, the skiff is rolling the other way.

Over and over again he tried all the tricks he had learned while swimming and playing water ball for raising his body in the water; and this for a moment would give him the purchase on the seal that was needed, but brought him no closer to success. Still the river was fighting him. And his strength seemed very little. As he rested, the seal lay quiet against him; but when cold and fatigue made his teeth chatter and his body shake, his distress communicated itself, and the small animal's eyes again were frightened. In spite of himself, Toivo sent another glance toward shore.

Somebody's built a fire over there, a big one, ran the thought through his head. Saturday-night picnickers, prob'ly. That's the kind of fire they make, big and bright. He could see the shapes of people moving about, some with lanterns. He set his teeth hard down on his lower lip to keep it from trembling. Those people were not about to leave their fun and come out here to help him—didn't even know he was there.

He'd best admit it: he was beaten. Best get away from here—so fast that he wouldn't hear the sound the little seal would make, knowing he was leaving it. A cold wind whipped him. Somewhere in his mind rose the thought of how good his shirt was going to feel on his back; and he avoided the seal's eyes when he spoke to him.

"Joe," he gasped, fighting for breath, not looking at the little face but seeing it anyway, "I tried as hard—as I could. You know? But I can't—get you into the boat —Joe." Abruptly he stopped speaking, for in his mind a discarded thought had stirred. He went back to pick it up. And suddenly he was full of hope!

"Funny Face!" He spat river water, tossed wet hair from his eyes. "Hold on! Hold on, boy!" One shaking hand held to the gunwale and he began with the other hand to tow the seal along with him, working his way back to the place where he had dropped his clothes in the boat.

His shirt! That was the thought that had come to him. His shirt would make a rescue sling for Joe!

TWO

It was not difficult, even while towing the seal, for Toivo to reach his shirt where it had fallen across the seat of the boat. In a few minutes he had the garment in his grasp and had worked his way back again to the boat's stern.

Now to tie the long sleeves of the garment around the young animal's body. This was something else again. Seals, Toivo decided, were made in the worst possible shape for harnessing. Joe was round in the middle, pointed at both ends.

"No hips on you, boy?" he inquired nonsensically, struggling with the problem of wrapping the shirt around the tapering seal, talking because his voice seemed to be important to Joe's morale—and that was about all the little guy had left to keep him alive. "No shoulders? How the dickens do you expect to hold your pants up, eh?"

Blowing often on his stiff fingers, Toivo worked against time and the cold water, against the young seal's weight and helplessness. Using his teeth, elbows, and chin to help hold and tie knots, he trod water, boosted Joe on a knee when he could, and worked at carrying out his plan.

22

He was trying to bring the two long sleeves of the shirt down, one to each side under Joe's front flippers. He wanted to cross the sleeves then under the belly, bring them forward and up, and tie them together at the back of the neck, where Joe no doubt had a collarbone.

The width of the shirt extended the reach of the sleeves and they'd go around all the way for sure. They could be tied on top. The trick was done.

"It's a sure thing now, boy!" the weary Toivo assured the seal, testing his knots one last time. The knots wouldn't slip. Good salty job. And the little animal's own weight pulling downward on the contraption should keep it from slipping off even those sloping shoulders.

Next thing now was to get his hands on the boat's painter; and for that he'd have to move forward. He thanked his stars that once he had carried it back again the length of the boat there'd be the extra iron ring at the stern to run it through. Most of the small craft along this section of the river had those stern rings. They kept your boat from banging around while at winter moorage.

I've got eighteen feet of rope there, his thoughts ran. The skiff's twelve feet long. Take out a bit for knots and still it will do. He paddled his way forward, again towing the little seal, picked up the free end of the coiled painter, and with the rope uncoiling its length behind him took his end of it back to the stern ring and ran it through. Joe made no trouble, didn't move.

"Tie the rope end at the top of the harness!" Toivo ordered himself. "Pick up the slack—want his face un-

der water? Run the bight through the ring, take two
half hitches—she's fast."

"We're on our way, Joe!" He looked closely at the
limp seal. Its half-open eyes held a faraway look. "Joe?"

He'd hurry! His thin shoulders flinched against the
evening chill as once again he bent to the rowing.

That fire onshore was brighter now. Some of the people swung lanterns down along the banks as if hunting
for something or signaling. Others were out in boats. He
could see the lights of three craft ahead of him and the
sails of at least two of them.

There still was no sound from the seal; but now and
again when a wave rode him high Toivo glimpsed his
little whiskered face and his big eyes. At least his eyes
were open, and he was coasting along all right back
there. What did the funny little animal think was happening to him? Toivo heard sounds upstream that made
him jerk his head, listen closely.

One of those boats up there was a motor, maybe five
horsepower, and it sounded like the *Gull,* his father's
boat, only that was crazy, because his father had said
he wouldn't be home. "Sunday is the same as any day
for me, when Saturday night's catch is to weigh," he had
said. And yet—that *was* the *Gull!* Toivo's oars moved
faster.

"TOIVO!" boomed Hadge Jarvenin's call across the
water, and the light from his boat shone in Toivo's eyes
so that he couldn't see. He stopped rowing, but after a
moment collected his wits and replied. "Ahoy!" (Blazes,
his voice had wobbled!)

"YOU FOLLOW! HEAR?"

"Okay!"

The *Gull* put about, pointing toward the cove; but before she proceeded, Hadge reached down and Toivo could see that he picked up the bull horn he always carried with him in the boat, and see his puffed cheeks as he sent three ear-splitting blasts of the horn bellowing through the darkness. That this was a prearranged signal was evident. The people at the bonfire now excitedly began to run toward one another, and two of the boats veered close to Toivo in the skiff. One on each side of him, sailing in close formation, lighting his way, they were like a Navy escort.

"Escort for an important person, by gar!" said Toivo to Joe. "For two important persons!" And suddenly, swiping the back of his hand across his eyes, he wished he could blow his nose. Then he heard somebody calling to him. Aarni.

"You giving shirts away today, Toiv?" the grinning big boy shouted, knowing well how cold his friend must be. "I'll take a few—long as you don't wear 'em any more!"

"Sure, Aarn!" Toivo's own grin returned full force. Wait! he thought. Just wait until he sees what's coasting along here with this boat.

"We expect a good story from you!" Mr. Ek shouted this. "Fellow who spends a whole day visiting mermaids!" Then came a voice that Toivo had not heard before, that of a stranger in Mr. Ek's boat.

"What I want to know," this voice asked of everyone else, and the tone was not that of joking, "is what kind of landlubbers do you raise on the river now—who go out without lights?"

"*Noh!*" ("Yes!") Everyone laughed, because everyone

25

was kind; but Toivo felt their reproach. "You said it! Hear that, boy?"

Right up to the door of the houseboat the teasing continued; then Toivo, his knees still shaking, stepped out onto the float and Mr. Ek saw all of a sudden where the skiff's painter was and what it was holding, and, quickly bringing another length of rope to make the skiff fast, took charge. Mr. Ek's own boat had been moored so that it hid Joe from the others, and Toivo saw that he would have to wait until another day after all to surprise Aarni, for the Rekkonens were leaving.

"Thanks!" he called to them, then included all around him, his tired grin flickering. "Thanks, everybody." They nodded, waved the words away.

"'S all right!"

The stranger with Mr. Ek, Toivo saw, was carefully drawing little Joe toward him, close to the edge of the float. Mrs. Ek, enormous as ever in her many skirts, her shawl and apron, stood, arms akimbo, in the doorway. His father had taken the *Gull* around to the other side of the float to moor her, but was coming now and had already seen Joe. Only Mrs. Ek of those left on the float had failed to spot the visitor. She was intent upon getting warmth and food to Toivo.

"Hot soup!" she called. "Come and get it!"

"Yes, ma'am." Toivo was at a loss now to know what to do with Joe. "I—I've got a seal with me."

"My stars!" The good lady craned her neck.

"It does not appear to be injured," announced the tall man who had examined the little seal, and he scrutinized Toivo too through his pince-nez.

"This is Doctor Smith," Mr. Ek explained. "Our cousin from Tillamook."

26

"There's something wrong with him, Doctor." Toivo looked up at this man's ruddy face and liked it. "He seemed to be drowning."

"Could be." Doctor Smith lifted the young seal gently to the dock. "Probably learned to swim not so very long ago."

"Seals have to learn?"

"They make little paddling motions right from the start, it is said. But even the human infant will often do that. People who have watched these fellows tell me that sometimes, either in fright or in an effort to hurry them along, their mothers push them into the water, and the youngsters are terrified kids for a while." The doctor now had untied the shirt harness; and he looked with appraisal at the boy next to him. "You know, you showed a lot of nerve, rigging that sling. Must have been quite a trick."

"Not—too much."

"Why don't you go on in, Toivo? Get your soup, and a jacket. We'll have a look at Mr. Whiskers."

"The jacket's here." Hadge had come around the corner of the house, had Toivo's coat in his hand. He cast a long, dark stare at Joe, then spat disgustedly.

"*Ei!* [No!] You are not stupid! You would not chance your life—for that?" He put the jacket about his son's shoulders, stood back, and folded his big arms. Toivo solemnly gazed at him and felt sorry for him. He knew his father's secret fear of the water. It came from a childhood in which an ear infection had prevented his learning to swim. This evening he had been badly frightened for his son.

"Guess I'd best stay out here," Toivo said, his gaze

locking with that of his father, "and help with the seal."

"Oh, I'll do it." Hadge threw up his hands in a what-else-can-I-do gesture. "Get your soup."

"He needs—"

"What he needs—he will *get!*"

"Okay." Toivo stumbled into the house.

Mrs. Ek kept giving reports from the doorway as she watched what went on outside and Toivo spooned up the good hot broth she had made for him.

"Cousin Eb—Doctor Smith—has gone over to the house for something," she announced. "Must be he needs his doctor bag. Your father's made a bed in a box for the young seal. The little critter don't appear to move."

"Eb's back again," she said a little while later. "He's —oh, dear! Using a sharp thing."

"Good." Toivo nodded. "Giving Joe a stimulant." He had felt when the doctor and Hadge carried the seal into the room in its box that chances already had improved for the little animal, for though its eyes still held the faraway expression, they were brighter.

"The main thing wrong with this youngster," Doctor Smith said, "is that he's starved. We'll get him warm and try to feed him. But I may as well warn you, boy. Don't count too much on saving him. He is pretty far gone."

"Even—if he eats?"

"Unlikely that he will eat. We'll try. Sam Ek has gone for some milk and a calf bottle."

"Poor queer little critter," Mrs. Ek murmured. "Lost and hungry."

28

"A sea lion," the doctor told her. "A pup. Probably less than three months old."

"Lion!" The large lady was startled.

"Just a name, Elin."

"You ever see one before, Eb?"

"Yes, but not up close. They are all along the coast here during this season. Belong to the eared seal family. Not the fur seals, but the hairy kind. Some—the smaller varieties—are used for trick acts in circuses. Others, larger, are probably just as intelligent; but they grow too big. This pup still wears his dark first coat; and I cannot tell if he will finish off with a California brown or the tan of our northern Steller sea lions." Toivo had been listening admiringly. He had always felt that to be a doctor was about the best thing a man could do with his life, and now was more convinced of this than ever.

"Joe could have been lost just today. Maybe it was his mother they shot at Astoria this morning," he said; but Eb Smith shook his head.

"Don't think so. He's been hungry longer than that. My guess is that he was orphaned some time ago, but may have been able to snatch a swallow or two now and then along with some other suckling pup, and has tried as long as he could to keep up with the herd. He is bone-thin and somehow—underdeveloped."

"He couldn't keep going any longer." Toivo touched the little round head of the sea lion. "He tried—awfully hard."

"It is difficult for a seal to drown, though this one would have done so after a while. They have automatic mechanisms in their noses and ears that close when their faces are under water."

"That's something. Automatic."

"Here comes the milk," Mrs. Ek announced; and Toivo ran to the door.

"In here, Mr. Ek!"

"Slowly now, Sam," warned the doctor; but Mr. Ek gave the bottle to him.

"You'd better do it," he said.

"Well, a whiff under his nose first, then, to let him know what it is. Then—probably a trickle on his lips to make him want it." The doctor suited actions to his words, but the sea pup did not respond. Its eyes looked far and beyond.

"Maybe some will go down from the corners of his mouth," said Doctor Smith, carefully spreading the dark lips with his thumb and finger. "That's a first-aid method with dogs." The warm drops flowed well back into the corners of Joe's mouth, but ran out at the other side; for he would not swallow.

"With people," offered the doctor, "you can sometimes do it this way." He took a teaspoon from the table, filled it with milk, then, while gently massaging the long stiff throat with one hand, again let drops flow into the mouth corners. Spasmodically Joe's lips pulled back. He bared his little sharp teeth, but did not swallow.

"For a calf," Mr. Ek suggested, "you hold your thumb down in a pail of warm milk to start off." Mrs. Ek fetched a pail, and they tried that. Mr. Ek said that he had got his thumb way up inside the sea lion's mouth; but it would not suck.

Hadge frowned. "Push him a little, so that he will have to do it." The big man poured milk back into the bottle, then pressed the rubber nipple hard against Joe's

30

unresponsive lips, moving it back and forth, letting the milk run; but slowly Joe's head fell to one side.

The doctor raised his eyebrows when he saw that, and shook his head; and the three men stood up.

"You have to—expect these things, Toivo, my boy," said the doctor. "I'm sorry." Toivo did not hear him. He had lifted the baby sea lion up onto his shoulder and was talking to him.

"Remember, Joe," he was saying, "what a fight you put up, out there in the river? And remember how you listened to me? You felt better when you heard me talking, didn't you? Well—you hear me talking now. You have to have food, same as I did. You have to stop acting like a baby when the time comes and be a big guy, see?" There was a faint movement of the eyes.

"*Wa-a-hoowr*," sighed Joe. Then, suddenly galvanized, he nuzzled into Toivo's neck. He humped his back and made impatient little sounds. And when Toivo gave him the bottle he bunted and jerked and scolded, but sucked it with some success.

"Well, what took you so long?" he seemed to be saying as his eyes sparkled. "Where've you been all the time?"

Toivo started to laugh; then, for the second time that night and in several years, was quietly crying.

The grown people looked at one another. Then, smiling, they shrugged their shoulders and all had a cup of coffee.

Hadge stood big and quiet for a moment beside Toivo's bed when Joe at last was settled in his box and the three of them were ready to have the light blown out.

"Good night, boy," he said. "It was bad for me—when I came home—and my son was not here."

Toivo dozed. For a moment before he went to sleep he had the thought that he must ask his father first thing in the morning how he happened to be there. What had changed his plans tonight and brought him home?

THREE

Only a few hours after he had dropped into sleep that first night with the young sea lion Toivo was awakened again by sounds in the room. Blinking, he raised himself on an elbow and gave his head a shake to rouse his senses. The sound seemed a complaining one, a muttering of discontented words. He could hear too a scratching and a slapping.

"Joe's out of his bed!" he said aloud, swinging his feet to the floor, feeling for matches. Hadge's shaggy head came up from his bunk at the other side of the room; and in the lamplight both of them blinked at the sea pup's cavortings.

To all appearances Joe was measuring the room and registering an objection to its smallness. He would stretch out full length as though to estimate a distance, then hump his back and pull his tail-end forward as a measuring worm does and make the trip around the room again and again.

"Too warm in here," said Hadge, amused in spite of himself.

"AH-HOWR!" agreed Joe.

"He might swim off if I put him outside." Toivo was uncertain. "He might—" Slap! Joe's flippers came down

33

onto the floor. He began to weave his sleek head and his neck—no longer stiff but now seemingly made of rubber—from side to side, muttering again his little "words" of disapproval, ready to win this argument.

"Well, he seems all right—not—delirious or anything." Toivo guessed maybe seals did prefer to be out-of-doors. After all, they must have warmer blood than people had, to be able to live in the places they were said to choose for homes; and tonight the temperature was merely cool along the river. He opened the door, and Joe humped himself out onto the moonlit float.

For a moment he looked at the water. Then he gazed at the sky. Shortly he began to rock his way around the house as though to make clear his claim to the place. Finally he sat still, fastened an expectant gaze upon Toivo, who had followed him, and waited.

"What are you trying to say, boy? Want your box out here?" Toivo dragged the box with its mattress of old canvas out through the door, while the young sea lion tipped his head this way and that, observing each step of the maneuver.

"Bet you think you could do it yourself, any time." Toivo laughed and dragged the box on around to the side of the house, placing it under the window that opened at the foot of his own bunk. Happily, as though this were precisely what he had ordered, Joe rocked over there and got into the box.

Shivering in the wind that had begun stirring, chuckling, Toivo made a dash for his own bed and pulled the blanket to his chin. Then, surprised, he blinked at the window; for there peering in at him was the little whiskered face he had just left.

34

"Okay, mister!" Toivo whispered, and, lifting a hand, put the tip of his thumb and the tip of his third finger together to make an all's-well sign. "Go to sleep."

The young seal flopped downward. He turned around a few times in his box. Then Toivo heard him make that sound which once had seemed to be a sigh, but which now was like secret laughter.

Hadge had the fire going early the next day. The good smell of fir pitch kindling and its cheerful crackle filled the room when Toivo opened his eyes. A quick look out the window told him that the little sea lion was still sleeping. He stretched pleasantly.

Everything was snug this morning, he thought. Father home, the breakfast cooking, and a long day ahead full of fun with Joe. Why was Father home, come to think of it? He'd be finding out at breakfast, probably. Idly he watched Hadge as he moved about the room. The big man stepped lightly, for all his size; his motions were neat and sure, never fumbling. When he lifted the stove lid to put in wood, the red flames lit his face; and there again he was different from most of the river men, for he was darker in coloring, did not have the flat, high look of the cheekbones, and his nose was narrower, his chin more angular than most of them. This morning, without the reindeer-hide cap to make his hair stick out at angles, the dark locks lay softly against his forehead. He must already have been to the sauna with Mr. Ek for his Sunday bath, for his hair was damp and he'd put on a clean shirt.

He's a handsome man. Why the dickens is somebody always telling me I look like him? Toivo sat up, met his own freckled reflection in the glass, and stuck out his tongue at it; then hunched his shoulders embarrassedly because he heard his father's laughter.

Hadge, stirring pancake batter, waved a small salute with his free hand, spoke in his native tongue as was usual when he and Toivo were alone.

"Your sea lion sleeps like a lamb."

"Guess he's not wriggled since he moved out there."

"We eat soon." Hadge put slices of salmon into a hot buttered skillet, broke an egg into the coffee to settle the grounds. "I'm leaving you alone for a longer time than I would ordinarily do. A chance to earn extra money downriver. I go at noon."

"Oh, no! Already?"

"Yes. For about four weeks. What would you say, though, if I told you that I shall not be going back many times more?"

"Hey!" Toivo began to jump into his clothes. He wanted to hear about this! "What's happened? Something good, or bad? Must be good, hm?" He never could tell a thing from his father's expression! And now the big man did not make any reply, merely took his time, served two plates with the scrambled eggs he had ready and the golden-brown fish, and set them on the warmer at the back of the stove.

"Have you washed, boy?"

"Going to!" Snatching a tin dipper from the wall, Toivo stepped outside, came in again with the dipper full of water, and emptied it into a basin on the bench near the stove. He reached for the yellow soap on a lard bucket lid on the bench, and began sloshing his face, neck, and ears into rosy cleanliness. His freckles stood out now more than ever. His red locks were in need of a comb, but he would not have stopped to apply it if his father had not motioned him back to the chore. With a last dab of the huck roller towel, he came to the table.

"Now. What's happened at the scow? Why won't you be going back there many more times?"

"The letter you brought out to me yesterday," Hadge said, setting the plates of food on the table and taking his own place, "was, as you know, from my brother."

"Sure. Uncle Urho in Hameenlinna."

"He thinks he has a buyer for the old place, and would like to come to this country, bringing his wife as I brought your mother, and to go into business here. He has the belief as I once had it—that this is the land of opportunity for his family."

"Why, that's great! When will he come?"

"Never. If I can stop him."

"I—must be stupid. This makes sense?"

"It makes sense. I came home to write the letter that will tell my brother his coming would be a mistake—as mine was a mistake—and to make it clear to him that if he does insist upon coming, he will not find me here."

"Still I don't see—" Toivo sighed. "Why won't you be here?"

"Because"—Hadge waited, let his words have all the drama his long pause could give them—"Hadge Jarvenin and son will be on their way back to the old country."

"A trip? Do we have money for that?"

"Not a trip. A journey back. Back to ways and people we know. A journey home. To Suomi."

"Not on your life!" Toivo jumped to his feet. His eyes flashed.

"SIT DOWN." Toivo sat. "The decision is made, Toivo."

"Suomi is—or was—your country, not mine!"

"She will take me back again. She will take my son. A brave, proud land can care for its own."

"Father, Finland is strange to me. You left there, remember? To make a better life. You're only thirty-four years old. Don't give up! I—I never thought you would be a—a quitter!"

Hadge gave him a long, hard look. "I am thirty-four and tired. You are not yet thirteen but already through the grades at the top of your class and ambitious to be a doctor. How about you? How shall you like to exchange that ambition—for a job on the fish scow? Tell me that!"

"I have no intention of—" Toivo's eyes widened.

"And I have no intention of letting you!"

"Funny." Toivo sagged in his chair, let his gaze go wandering over the room and back to Hadge. "Just a little while ago, when I woke up, I was thinking that it was snug in here."

"All we have"—Hadge Jarvenin frowned darkly—"is the security of a day's wages. Nothing more. And what solution do you have to offer, since you see fit to object to mine? What way do you suggest to get us out of this trap that holds us? Eh?"

"I don't know! It's all coming at me too fast!" Even to his own ears Toivo's voice sounded shaken; and suddenly the need to be away and alone overcame him.

"I'll get fresh water for us!" he cried, and hurried out the door. He'd get some milk too.

Hardly had he picked up the two pails from the deck outside and headed across the runway toward shore when he heard young Joe coming behind him. The little sea lion's rocking-horse gait was urgent; his outstretched neck showed his anxiety at being left by himself.

"Hi!" Toivo's spirits could not help lightening at this sight. Here was company he welcomed. "So you are awake. And hungry again? You think you're going someplace?" Joe did not reply, but swung alongside, keeping pace, and began bump-bump-bumping the pail that last night had contained warm milk. "Know what you want, don't you, and where we got it? Maybe I'd best not let you learn where milk comes from in the first place, then. You once catch the idea that cows donate this stuff and I'll bet you'd decide to tackle a cow and help yourself!"

They came to a small enclosure around the spring that was the water supply for the Eks and Jarvenins. Here Joe tipped his head, watched Toivo swing a leg over the lower fence rail and slide through; then he himself slithered neatly under the rail and waited to see what came next. Toivo washed both the pails he had brought, intending to fill one of them with water and set it outside the fence to pick up on his way home; but something made him postpone doing this. Joe's skin seemed dry and Toivo thought that this was not the way a sea lion should look.

Slowly, making sure that the little animal approved of the maneuver, he began to pour water over Joe's head and back. Joe looked blissful. He batted his eyes, wriggled his tail-end, waggled himself at both ends and in the middle, and almost rushed his friend into the spring, trying to get more.

"AH-HOOWR!" cheered Joe. "Blazes, that feels good!"

"Okay." Toivo refilled the pail and set it outside the fence. "We'll do that lots of times." Now he'd go for the milk.

Through the open upper half of the barn door Toivo could hear, as he came close, the rhythmic tattoo of crisscross streams of milk hitting a pail, and he knew that Mr. Ek already was busy. He could look down the length of the barn, see the horses, Dick and Bonnie, at the far end next to the tool room, their brown necks arched over their grain boxes, and the three cows in stalls nearer to him, where Bingo and Yellow One, the Eks' dog and cat, waited for breakfast in their own special way.

Toivo wasn't sure if he should let his pet come on into the barn, but, since the young seal himself appeared hesitant, thought probably Joe would not venture farther than the entrance. The greedy pink tongues of the cat and dog already were licking their noses in anticipation of what was to come, and this was always a show worth watching.

With a glance in Bingo's direction to get his aim right, Mr. Ek now turned a stream of milk through the air from the cow's udder to the dog. Like a flash, Bingo lifted to his haunches, caught a large share of the milk in his mouth, and gulped it down with satisfaction. The little man then aimed a stream in the direction of the cat; and she grew frantic trying to stretch her tiny pink mouth wide enough to gobble it all; but at the end gained most of her satisfaction by pawing away from her own little chin the white festoon of milk that hung there, and neatly licking her paws.

"That won't stop them." The watching boy grinned. "They'll go right along to the next station and be ready for another handout." Neither he nor Mr. Ek nor the cat or dog was looking Joe's way; but suddenly—all at the same moment—they were aware of him!

It was when the little sea lion rocked forward to gain a better view of this new way of serving breakfast that they all noticed him.

The dog barked. He growled and snarled and made lunges. The cat wailed and spat, jumped up on a stanchion and glared. Down the barn the horses whinnied, kicked, and whirled in their box stalls; and the startled cows kicked, upsetting a full pail of milk to roll like a white flood across the barn floor.

"Mr. Ek! Help me!" Toivo shouted. "Get the dog away from Joe!" But little Mr. Ek's face was alert. He had stood perfectly still after his first surprised jump; and now spoke soothingly, his eyes on the sea lion.

"Hold it," he said. "Boy, your critter don't need help. He's handling things okay." Toivo caught his breath. This was true!

Joe had erected for himself a double line of defense. He had backed his rear end in between the wall and a barrel of grain so that nothing of him was within an enemy's reach except his sharp teeth and the lightning strikes he made with them; but he was not striking to hurt, only to warn.

Oh, look, now, he seemed to be saying to Bingo in a

more or less reasonable manner, you notice, I'm sure, that I am not using these teeth, only showing them? Why don't you relax, friend? I'm a visitor here, just passing through.

Friend? Bingo was accustomed to friends. Besides, his boss was quietly assuring him that all was well. He stopped barking, tipped his head, and looked Joe in the eye, then went back to wait another turn at milk catching. And the cat, on soft, swift feet, crossed over to sit beside the dog. Then Joe the sea lion, bright and eager, rocked to his own place in the lineup.

"Toivo?" There was something almost like reverence in Mr. Ek's hushed voice; and Toivo swallowed before he could speak.

"I'm—looking. Go ahead, Mr. Ek—try him."

Carefully, slowly, the little man resumed his milking. He turned the stream of milk through the air again; first to the dog's mouth; then to the cat's. Then casually he aimed the milk at Joe, whose great wise eyes were watching. That young sea lion shifted his head a fraction of an inch to correct the aim, opened his mouth like a catcher's mitt, and neatly gulped down the white stream without losing a drop of it!

"It was millions of years ago," stated Mr. Ek in the voice of a sleepwalker afterward, when he and Toivo had come outside. "I read about it once. Critters like Joe were land animals then, the piece said; only they got scared off somehow and took to water." He drew a long breath. "Now—this one, he comes back. And it's as if he—as if he remembers! Some part of him already knows things." The little man shrugged. He jerked his mind back to business. "How about it? Want any milk today?"

"Don't know if you can spare it after that spill."

"Yep."

"Well, I'd like to do some work—to pay for the spill."

"Would?" Mr. Ek was always agreeable to offers like this.

"In fact—" A new idea popped into Toivo's head. He thought perhaps he had the answer to his father's problem. "In fact, Mr. Ek, I'd like to apply to you for a regular job as helper!"

"For the summer, I s'pose you mean."

"Summer, winter, all the time. I'd try hard to do things right."

"I believe that. Let me think a minute. Your pa willing? Ain't you going to high school?"

"Sure, Mr. Ek! I'm going to high school just as soon as I can make it there! I'm saving every cent I can get for that."

"Yes. Boy like you wants to go to school." Mr. Ek took a few uncertain steps; recalled something he had almost forgotten. "Oh. Eb Smith left a message for you. Said he'd turned up a couple more items in his mind about seals. Said he read somewhere you have to keep their eyes from getting dry or they can go blind. And he said that this kind of seal that he thinks yours is, Steller, well—they grow awful all-fired big."

"Thanks." Toivo's heart was thankful that he had poured water over little Joe. And he was regretful that some sea lions grew terribly large. But right now those two facts were beside the issue. "How about my job, Mr. Ek?"

"Well now, look. I'll teach you anything I know—milking, how to mix feed, gardening, and such. And I'd enjoy having your help. But—do you think you could take a meal a day as part payment?"

"Yes, *sir!*" Toivo's spirits soared. Take Mrs. Ek's good cooking? Couldn't he, though!

"Father can go now, if he wants to, Joe," he told the young seal, on the way home, "without worrying about me. He's free! And you and I, old Funny Face—you and I will stick together! Through thick and thin, hm?"

"Suits me fine," Joe told him with lolloping, cheerful unconcern. "Anything you do, Toivo, always suits me." The two of them burst in where Hadge, still seated at the table, was carving one of the small figurines he enjoyed making. He did not look up.

"Father—"

"You are back, I see."

"I have some news. Good news—to tell you. I've a job—working for Mr. Ek—and you are free to go back to Finland—if you want to—because you won't have to worry about me." It was a long and breathless announcement, but the silence following it was longer. When Hadge did at last lift his face and look at his son, Toivo was as usual unable to read his expression; but his voice when he spoke had the politeness of a stranger.

"Thank you," he said. "You have *sisu* [spirit]. You may be a better Finn than you think."

"I—I'll be getting a good meal each workday, and—"

Hadge interrupted him by rising and picking up his oilskin, his lunch—and the Laplander cap. "A son's home," stated Hadge Jarvenin stiffly, "is his father's

44

house." He paused at the door, pulled on the cap. Rent and grocery money are here on the table."

"We'll be fine."

"*Hyvaa.* [Good.] Now get that sea pup weaned off milk as soon as you can. And get rid of it." He was gone.

"*Get rid of it!*" Toivo stood a long time staring at the floor, hearing the sound of the *Gull's* motor fainter and fainter down river. "*Rid of Joe?*"

Aimlessly he wandered about the room, moved the clock, picked up some photographs and looked at them, finally slipped a wax cylinder on its spindle and wound the gramophone. A violin solo, "Humoreske," filled the house.

Almost at once Joe turned his head, his big eyes pleased and whiskers lifted in curiosity. Then he made a sound somewhere inside him as his body seemed to shiver and began to sway his head in the short, staccato rhythm of the music.

"Hey!" Toivo forgot for a moment his earlier distress. "You can keep time like a person! Like that piece, hm?" Joe's face was full of mischief. He had no time for conversation, but continued his head bobbing until the music ended.

"That's Father's favorite!" Toivo was excited. "We'll put on your show for him. Joe!" But Hadge's parting words came to haunt him once more: *The sea pup—get rid of it.*

He turned away from the machine, a painful lump in his throat. "Joe," he said, looking into the intelligent eyes of the now quiet young animal, touching the round head and the soft throat, "boy, we are in trouble!"

FOUR

Toivo started his chores for Mr. Ek the following week.

"Five days a week we'll make it," the little man said, "from six to noon, with dinner and a dollar a week, if that's okay. But Saturdays and Sundays, those are days when a boy your age should be doing the things a boy was meant to do—swimming and fishing and that."

"You don't know how much I like working here." Toivo was warmed as always by the kindness of this man and of his big wife. "Planting stuff and taking care of the animals—doesn't seem like work." He decided, though, that he would keep the two free days. After all, there was Joe to think of. Joe must be taken swimming every day. The young sea lion, as it turned out, felt equal responsibility for looking after Toivo.

Swimming, rowing, fishing, treasure hunting. No longer were these the occupations of a lonely boy who kept wishing he were "up at the Rekkonens" or that the Rekkonen kids were down with him; for Joe the adventurer was with him now in everything he did, and everything was fun because of that little clown. Toivo could almost forget his father's cold anger with him in the closer emotion of joy in each day's living; and before August came to an end Hadge's threat to leave his adopted country had faded into unreality.

Toivo loved the harvest colors and smells as the season wore on; and he and Joe together reveled in the products of autumn. Long, twisted squashes yellowing in the sun out by the barn became baked delicacies topped by butter and brown sugar, or one-crust spicy pies; tomatoes that glowed like red jewels in a showcase of leaves and vines turned into cool salads—or sweet preserves; corn, in the hottest spot on the hill back of the house day by day grew more ready for the table; and the concord grapes with which Mr. Ek had long been experimenting by September had begun to bulge and drip their luscious purple juice. Certainly Joe ate none of these. But he understood well that Toivo valued them, and appeared to encourage his frequent samplings.

I don't know which is better, the boy would think, the mornings with Joe on the farm or the afternoons with Joe along the river. The next weeks lay ahead of him, a dream of golden days, and he would not look back or beyond them.

"Fruits and vegetables got to be brought in, boy," Mr. Ek told him, "even if you do think they look so fine out there. Fruit-and-root cellar's a-waitin'." He and Toivo began the task of storing the fall harvest for winter use, and Mrs. Ek's kitchen as she took over her own share of preparation began issuing aromas of canned preserves and pickles.

"It's good, Joe—a kind of safe feeling—to own a piece of the earth that produces for you," Toivo told his seal. Awareness like this, of the goodness of the earth, and a sense of permanence and peace while working close to it, had been one of the rewards of his friendship with Mr. Ek. Work with farm animals, he had found, gave him the same assurance, for they had trusted him.

"You have good hands," Mr. Ek told him, "strong and gentle. The kind of hands for a good farmhand—or a doctor."

"Gentle maybe," Toivo had told him in a slightly woebegone way in those first few days of learning, "but not strong enough to get a stream of milk from a cow."

" 'Twon't take long. You'll see."

Now he had learned to milk, and was permitted to take over as his own on the days when he was working the milk-catching routine of the cat, dog, and sea lion. As long as he lived, he was sure, he would find delight in thinking of those three little animals in their daily act of catching milk in midair.

They can't be anything alike or related in any way so far as their ancestors go, he often thought as he whistled in the morning for Bingo, Yellow One, and Joe and the three came galloping to their places in line beside one of the cows. And yet they are alike in a lot of ways. All of them had quick adaptability to the ways of human beings; each of the three had a need to be thought well of; and all of them were overflowing with wonderful clownish fun.

Each night after he had given Joe his bottle of milk, just before they both dropped off to sleep, the boy would look at the young seal and think happily of the three pets and of how they would welcome him in the morning. Then he would turn his thoughts for a few moments as always to his father, hoping all was well with him.

It had not been easy at first to get Joe to return to the water. Whether this was because he recalled his near drowning and was afraid, or had reverted to a lost baby-

48

hood, or thought that Toivo might be trying to lead him away from his new home was not clear; but for the first two days of his life on the houseboat he refused to swim. He would neither dive from the float when Toivo dived nor be coaxed to walking into the river from the beach. Recalling Doctor Smith's warning about the danger of dry eyes, Toivo poured gallons of water over the little animal, and for two entire afternoons divided his efforts between diving from the float to prove to Joe that this was safe and coaxing him from below to jump into the water.

I'm not going into that river, Joe seemed to be thinking. And I don't want that boy of mine in there, either. And he did everything possible to show his disapproval of the whole idea.

When Toivo was in the water below him, the sea-lion pup would slide back and forth, right and left, along the edge of the float, crying and scolding at the top of his voice. Sometimes he leaned so far out over the water in his anxiety and wish to pull Toivo back up to him again that it seemed that his weight and his outstretched head and shoulders would surely overbalance him and he would come tumbling down; but never did this happen.

On that third day Toivo had tried a trick. Instead of coaxing, urging, "Come on, Joe boy," as he had been doing, he dived in without a word to Joe and began to swim upstream away from the float, as though intending to leave the seal behind; and his trick worked. Joe went wild.

"*Ah-woohr!*" he wailed. "Can't you see me? AH-WOOHR!" He was able to see only his boy's retreating back; but Toivo, by swimming at an angle, could watch

49

operations over one shoulder, and he saw that, sure enough, Joe refused to be left.

Flippers folded back, long neck outstretched, that sea pup flashed from the float to the water in as clean and beautiful a dive as ever the river had witnessed. Toivo cheered, and came back. Now the fun could begin! He waited for Joe to come up from his dive.

It took a long moment; but then there Joe was, his face not far from Toivo's, his big eyes sparkling. Looking into those eyes, the thought came to the boy that they were not so blue as they had been, but were changing to brown.

"You're growing up!" He splashed water into the whiskered face, and Joe took another dive. Down there in the sunlit water he seemed a darting phantom, a swift and graceful shadow. Joe, it was plain to be seen, could keep his eyes open under water better than Toivo could do it after all his long practice, and could swim faster, turn more sharply, dive deeper, and stay under longer than any boy ever would be able to do. In water, Joe was neither funny nor awkward.

Smack! Water splashing his own face interrupted Toivo's thoughts, made him catch his breath and dodge; then he laughed, for he understood. Joe was acting in imitation of the teasing he had received from his swimming friend only a few minutes earlier.

"We're even!" Toivo began to swim back toward home. "Hold it, Joe!"

Good, the sea pup appeared to be thinking, looking smug. Then he swam under and to either side of his boy, raced ahead of him and back again. Glad you're using some sense. You are really not too good at this swimming business, you know, Toivo. I'll always have to be right close, to look out for you.

"Fine thing!" Toivo was ready to laugh aloud at the way the seal was behaving, but held back because this might hurt Joe's feelings. Old Funny Face has forgotten, he said to himself, that he had to be helped out of swimming troubles of his own—not very long ago.

On that first night that Hadge was away Joe had moved back inside the house to sleep. The door had been open and the room was cool. Toivo was trying to waken enough to reach for a blanket when it happened. Only half understanding at first, he had blinked at a shape standing silently beside his bed. Joe. How long had the little sea lion been standing there waiting for him to waken? It seemed to him when he lit the lamp that the wishful whiskered face looked tired.

"What are you trying to say, Funny Face?" he'd asked him. "Want to sleep in here while Father's away? That it?" He had pushed the kindling box close to his bed to make a step up; and Joe (about as graceful as a boy would have been with his feet tied together and boxing gloves on his hands), had clambered aboard, to sleep there ever since.

I don't know for sure, Toivo had thought, grinning in the dark, whether he is lonesome—or thinks I am. He had not hugged or much caressed the young animal, but had given him rather the companionship of his voice; for he sensed in this creature from the sea a wild compulsion, even with all his adaptability, to keep between himself and man one last barrier. At night sometimes, however, he did have to push Joe's weight off his feet.

He's not so thin any more, he began to say to himself as the days and nights went by. He's growing. And the sleepy thought would drift through his mind: Wonder how big sea lions do get to be, anyway?

When Hadge had been gone for a month Toivo felt that his precious carefree interlude was over, that now he was going to have to face his problems and could no longer look the other way. The reality of his father's need to escape from perpetual discouragement must be faced, and the extent of his anger with his son who had called him a "quitter." The fact that no plans had been made for his own high-school work when winter came must be admitted—and somehow corrected. And then—then the fact must be faced that Joe was still here and that Toivo loved and needed the little animal, and had no intention of getting rid of him.

"What a mess." Toivo's frowning gaze went out the door and back to meet Joe's eyes watching him. Then he swung his feet to the floor.

"But don't worry, boy." He went to the stove, began to lay the fire. "Something will work out. It's got to work out for us." He gave the seal his breakfast, drank his own coffee without interest, then sat out on the float with his back braced against the side of the house and tried carefully to sort out thoughts that he had been pretending were not in his mind.

I shouldn't have said what I did to Father, I know. And yet—it seemed that I had to speak what I felt. I only wish I'd been a little more polite about it. Wonder what he said in his letter to Uncle Urho—if he wrote the letter. I didn't see it anywhere. Wonder what kind

52

of a mood he'll be in when he gets home? Restlessly he re-entered the house and walked about. Joe continued to watch him. It actually isn't much of a house—not the kind of home Father planned. Suddenly he saw the room as it actually was: cramped, untidy, dirty. Why, he had even let Joe sleep on his blankets without a canvas to protect them, and they were oily, stained dark from the young animal's skin. Blazes! This was no sort of place for a man to come home to!

Toivo began to think, as he pushed back the table, pulled forward the wash bench and tub, reached for hot water, of the way things used to be. Maybe after he'd got the house cleaned he could cook up something to have ready for his father to eat—something he liked— the way Mom used to do.

She had a way of preparing salmon, he remembered— "*suolakalaa,*" she called the dish. How his father enjoyed that! And she served it with rye-dough bread rings that she had dried by running them onto a pole between the rafters of her shining kitchen. His father had always had a certain way of coming into that kitchen, he remembered, hurrying, as though he could hardly wait to find himself there. Maybe, Toivo thought, if I had tried harder to keep this place decent, Hadge Jarvenin would be more like himself right now, more willing to tackle problems—and not so willing to give up. He snatched the yellow soap, poured hot water into the tub, realized he needed spring water for cooling it.

"Joe, listen. Will you stay here this time, wait for me to get back? I'm in a dickens of a hurry!"

"Nope." Joe thought not. He hadn't checked the calendar and did not know that this was Saturday, a day off, and could see no reason why they should not both be on their way to the barn and the milking. Certainly he would not stay behind. Toivo didn't have the heart to close the door on him.

"Come on, then," he said grudgingly. "But behave. Hear?" And on the way to the spring he explained exactly what the situation was: that Hadge would be home, that he would undoubtedly be full of worry about his problems, and that Joe the sea pup was not going to be to him the most welcome of sights. Joe listened, unimpressed.

You do make speeches! his humorous glances in Toivo's direction might have been saying. But why bother? You and I have another fine day ahead of us, boy!

Toivo had to take time to pour water over the insistent little sea lion's back and time to pick up a pail of milk from the farmhouse porch, and then time to coax the unwilling young Joe home again. And of course once they were back he had to take time to give Joe more milk. And suddenly, after all this, he looked with new eyes at the lively young fellow and knew that he was foolish to be doing any of these things for him.

"You know something?" he said. "You don't need these shower baths any more. You have the whole Columbia River to bathe in." Joe's fuzzy face turned toward him reproachfully. "And how about this nursing-bottle routine? Isn't it time you started eating fish?"

"*Ah-woohr,*" admitted Joe guiltily, ducking his head, sounding as if he said, "It's your own fault."

"I know. Guess I never offered any to you because as a matter of fact I was afraid to admit you are that old and

54

can eat real food." Toivo sighed. His father's "Now get that sea pup weaned off milk, and get rid of it," seemed to echo through the house.

He emptied the cold water into the hot water now, brought in the washboard from its nail outside, again reached for the yellow soap. One by one he pulled the blankets from both the beds and scrubbed them clean, then washed all the soiled pieces of clothing, the towels, everything. After sloshing them again in clear water he draped them over the lines in the sun.

Tired but still determined to do all things possible to put Hadge in a good humor and to let him know his son cared for him, as always, Toivo now scrubbed all surfaces both inside and outside the house, brought in the sun-dried clothes, made the beds fresh and smooth. It was sundown when the work was done.

Now for the big surprise, the final offering: the money in the old sugar bowl. Toivo had been adding to this secret hoard for a number of years all his birthday-gift money and most of everything he had earned, and it was intended to help get him started in high school; but now he felt that Hadge's need for help was very great and that his desperation must be eased. There was fourteen dollars in that bowl. And another four dollars to add to it, which he had earned, working for Mr. Ek.

He regretted that the clock told him it was too late to go to the store and that he had not been able to cook something good, but never mind. They would get along well enough tonight, and tomorrow, since the store-keeper lived in the same building with his business, they would be able, even though it was Sunday, to get their supplies.

"Wow!" Toivo flopped down at the table to rest and looked around approvingly at the clean house. "Think he'll like this, Joe?" Joe did not answer. He had not made a sound in a long time, and he didn't make any now. Toivo turned to look at him and saw that he wasn't there.

He wasn't in the house or outside on the float, and he wasn't in the river, having a swim. He was not anywhere in sight!

It will soon be too dark to find him! I'd better get help! Toivo darted across the planking toward shore and Mr. Ek's house, came to an uncertain halt, began again to run—and stopped short, his pulse thumping; for he had heard the sound of the *Gull's* engine. His father's boat was close by!

FIVE

The sound of the *Gull's* engine told Toivo that his father's boat was only a few minutes away. He needed more than minutes! If Joe were hurt, helpless somewhere, it might take a long time to find him.

I'll have to meet the boat, though! After the way Father felt—and what I said to him—he'll think I don't care about him if I run off. This thought turned him back.

But no—Joe needs help! Once more he changed direction.

"Joe!" he shouted, running. "Where are you?"

Some sound came to him. It was from the end of the planking. He halted to listen, whistled the call he always used when summoning the three pets at milking time in the mornings; and now also it brought an answer. From below the end of the walkway, where water was shallow but mud deep at this tide, there came the sound of Joe's splashing and a muffled "word" from him.

"You there?" Toivo leaped toward the sounds. "Hey, something wrong?"

His sea lion stood high, facing him. And tight, tight for a moment, the boy closed his eyes against the vision. From nose to bigger flippers Joe was encased in mud.

He seemed to be grinning with excited, triumphant impudence, and gripped in his teeth was a flapping salmon. Toivo groaned.

"You've done it this time! The last minute of the last hour of the last day Father's gone you prove he's right to claim you're a nuisance! He will be pleased—real pleased—with both of us." Behind the fish, Joe's grin widened. He lolloped forward, made loud coughing and wheezing sounds with his throat and full mouth, cascaded mud behind him. Close by at the moment—almost in—Toivo heard the motorboat throttling down.

"*You stay there*," he shouted to his seal, spinning away floatward, "*and swallow that thing!*" Struck with astonishment, Joe did just that.

Tide's out, thought Toivo, speeding. Father'll land below. He skimmed the ladder like a fireman on a pole, skidded to a halt at the float's edge as the *Gull* glided the last few yards toward him under momentum. That was the way to bring her in. Hadge had taught him to do this too.

Then he saw that it was not Hadge Jarvenin who was coming in. The navigator of the little craft was Ab Rekkonen, who cupped his hands to his mouth and shouted as soon as he was near enough.

"Your pa wants some clean clothes. Can you find some?" His broad face looked up pleasantly. "Got to go on up to the house, get me some gear too." Toivo's knees felt likely to buckle and he wished that he had someplace to sit down. What a joke—a joke on him, with his silly surprises. Only he didn't feel like laughing.

"I thought he was coming home!" he managed to call back to Mr. Rekkonen after a moment.

58

"Had to work. Both of us. Chance to make extra pay."

"Sure."

"Think you might find some stuff for him?" Ab's glance sharpened as he waited for an answer. "Toivo?"

"Oh. Yes. Just a minute." He went up the ladder and back into the shining-clean house where the sugar bowl and its gift of his savings waited on the table, put clean underwear, pants, and shirt in a flour sack and carried this down to his friend. Mr. Rekkonen reached a paper up to him as he took the clothes.

"Note from your pa," he said.

"I'll read it in the house." Toivo squinted his eyes at the gathering darkness and shoved the paper into his pocket. "Everything is—all right, though, isn't it?"

"*Kaikki kunnossa* [Everything's fine]."

"Good."

"I was wondering"—Mr. Rekkonen seemed to Toivo to be considering him with special attention, and to become suddenly, rather loudly, cheerful—"why don't you row up to the place tomorrow? I'll tell the missus to expect you for dinner."

"I'd like that."

"The seal still here?"

"Yes." Toivo wondered if Hadge had asked for the answer to this question. "He's here." *He's here,* his thoughts added, *gobbling a fish!*

"Good. The kids'll have a workout with him." Ab backed away, put the *Gull* about, and pointed her upstream toward his home, while Toivo waved his thanks. He took his father's note then and went inside to read it. But hardly had he trimmed the lamp and settled into a chair when he was interrupted by someone at the door.

Mr. Ek and another man stood there. Toivo always wondered afterward when he happened to recall the episode if his sudden anger came entirely from the fact that the stranger with Mr. Ek was holding a shotgun at a threatening angle or if perhaps this was the finale of a long, hard day.

"I'm awfully sorry, boy," Mr. Ek was saying, stepping into the room followed by the other man, "but we got trouble. When he"—a big thumb indicated his companion—"went back to his boat tonight after talking some business up at the house he—well, I guess Joe had been into things."

"Ruined my jacket!" exploded the stranger. "Smeared my boat from here to hell—stole my fish!" His furious eyes searched the room. "Where's he at?"

"Where he is," stated Toivo coldly, looking hard at the shotgun, "is somewhere else."

"I *told* him Joe's a pet." Mr. Ek pushed at the man's gun. "Put that thing down!"

"Just tell me—where's the devil at?"

Toivo felt sick. He felt something else too. And Mr. Ek, who knew well what Hadge Jarvenin's reaction would have been to a situation of this kind, could see the same chill in Toivo's eyes.

"You are in this house, mister," stated Toivo with controlled fury, "not invited, with a loaded gun in your hands. That makes you a criminal. If you don't want to face arrest, you get out of here—*now*."

The man stepped back, but still glowered.

"Your fish will be paid for," Toivo continued, beginning to close the door. "And I'll be out there in a shake and clean your boat. But, mister, don't ever point a gun at me again, or point one at my seal."

"Bring a lantern, Toiv," Mr. Ek called over his shoulder, urging his companion to depart. "I'll help you."

"I'll be there," Toivo told him, "with two lanterns." His hands shook, he could see that, while he filled the lanterns and got them ready; but this, he assured himself, was because he needed food and not for any other reason. When he closed the door on his way out he saw that his father's message still lay on the table, unread.

Where was the young sea lion now? In his mind's eye he could still vision the mud-splashed little robber with the fish in his grinning mouth.

"Joe," Toivo whispered, hurrying along the planking, his heart beating a painful tattoo in his chest, "stay away from here. Keep out of sight—until this is over, *please?*" The two men and the mud-smeared boat were waiting for him at the end of the runway.

Later, ravenous for a meal, cold, and muddy from tip to toe as Joe had been, Toivo dragged himself homeward. With Mr. Ek's good help order had been brought to the stranger's boat. And the man's anger had cooled enough so that he declined payment for the fish.

"Willing to drop the whole thing," he said to Toivo, "if you forget the business with the gun. Got to admit I made a mistake there."

"If you say so." Toivo was already on his way.

"But you'd better watch that seal!" Not too easily could the man let things go. "Somebody'll get him!" The light on his boat bobbed away in the darkness and for a moment Toivo watched it.

61

That's one thing you're right about, he said to the man in his thoughts. Too darned right.

He followed the muddy trail that Joe had left; and it led, as he'd thought it would, directly to the box under the window and to Joe, soundly sleeping there, his middle section bulging as it had never bulged before.

"You heard everything that went on," whispered Toivo, reaching a hand to stroke the round head; and Joe, awakening, but pretending not to be awake, peered at him from guilty, half-shut eyes. "You aren't fooling me." He had meant to be severe, but felt only sad and terribly tired. This day and this evening had marked a turning point for both of them. For him, there'd been the hours of fact facing and the realization that he might not be able to find answers to his problems. For Joe, there had been a first meal of solid food and the first time he had gone to bed of his own accord. Little Joe was no longer a baby sea lion; he was a growing boy.

Like me, thought Toivo. And both of us—sort of lost in the shuffle. He went in to read Hadge's message. It was a hurried one, written in Finnish, with a pencil.

Explain to the Eks [it directed] that I will be away for another week because of extra work at the cannery, and that I shall appreciate their waiting that long for the rent and milk and egg money. [Always so anxious to pay his way on time, thought Toivo.] This extra work will go a long way toward springing that trap we spoke of. I know you will be all right, but keep in close touch with the Eks.

Hadge Jarvenin.

Toivo crumpled the paper and threw it in the wood box.

"Sounds as if he's about ready to leave the country! As if he'd never given a thought to what I said or how I feel—as if he didn't even hear me." He stood for a moment staring at the room he had spent the day cleaning in a childish effort to please his father. Then he stepped to the window and looked out at Joe.

"What shall I do?" he whispered to the night; and asked again of the empty room, "What shall I do?" Slowly he sank into a chair. *"What can I do?"* His head went down on his arms on the table.

He knew when he lifted his head after a while that he had slept, and he felt better, but needed food. Bacon and eggs, he thought; that would do it. And milk. He cooked the food, wolfing it down, not bothering with a plate, stacked skillet and mug to be washed some other time, and put water to heat for a bath.

"I'm dirtier than Joe was. That's a fact." Rest and food had begun to revive him, and he brightened at the thought of a warm soaking. He'd do the full routine, he decided; he'd take the royal road to cleanliness, by means of the most efficient method so far discovered. This required certain definite preparations.

"First," he proclaimed to imaginary listeners, "you lay out in a row all the stuff you need: soap, washcloth, towel." He placed these properly. "You put the tub on the floor the right distance from the stove so you get the heat, and you pour in hot water, then cold water, until it feels good." Here, he tested the water with a big toe, nodded his head. "And now"—he sat down in the hot water, his long legs hanging over the tub's edge and

pointed toward the stove—"ah-hh!" Food, sleep, and a
hot bath. You couldn't beat those for solid comfort. Not
in any country. The combined heat of water and stove
went through him deliciously; his worries floated off on
the fragrance of yellow soap; and lazy thoughts flowed
in and out of his mind.

"So Father really wants to go back to the old country," he mused as one not vitally concerned with the fact
and not worried about it. "Says it's a fine country, his
Suomi, full of brave people; and of course it is. Every
grade-school kid knows that Finland has always had to
be standing up to somebody or other. But—" He broke
off here. It was time to rinse. And this was important.

"Now the rinsing," he stated in a showman's voice to
his imaginary listeners, "is where the efficiency comes in.
The point is—do all your rinsing at one time, the same
time when your feet are getting clean." He now stood
up, stepped back into the tub with both feet in the water, and assumed a squatting position, then reached for
the washcloth, dipped it in the water, and repeatedly
squeezed it over his well-soaped head and the rest of
him, until the streams of water had washed away all
soap.

"And there you have it!" He stood in front of the
stove, rubbed himself dry with a rough towel, and could
not help grinning a little at his own nonsense and because he felt so good.

You know, he told himself, this might just be a smart
idea to use when he was a doctor. It would save a lot
of pills!

"You just eat your groceries," he'd say to those patients who were full of worries but otherwise all right,

"and take lots of baths. I guarantee that your problems will go up in steam and melt with the soap." He sat for a moment on the edge of his bunk his thoughts sobering.

At least Father's plans are farther away again, he told himself sleepily. A lot can happen—he might even somehow change his mind.

The clean bedding felt good to him as he stretched on his bunk. It smelled good too, full of soap and fresh air. He would worry no more, but think of tomorrow with the kids. Tomorrow was going to be a dilly of a day.

Into his mind came pictures of the Rekkonen children: the littlest one, Sis (Selina), with her skinned-back pigtails and her affectionate, toothless smile, her two round-headed brothers with their cereal-bowl haircuts and blue eyes of mischief. They made every day good for each other. He'd get up early, he told himself comfortably. He'd fish a bit to get a breakfast for Joe, and give Joe a brushing before they went upriver. He hoped that the sea pup would show the kids his best tricks—and that he wouldn't get into any trouble.

Reaching to turn down the lamp wick, he puckered his mouth to blow out the flame but did not at once draw the breath for it; for there at his window a face again looked in at him, a whiskered face, and it was sad.

"It's okay, Joe." Toivo lifted a hand, made their signal. "All kids have to grow up." The sad look slid away from the face; the eyes twinkled.

With a flip, Joe threw himself backward into his box; and Toivo heard him for a few minutes after the light was out, happily hunkering down.

SIX

"Hi, in there! Anybody goin' fishin'?" That was Sam Ek's call at 5:30 the next morning; and it started Toivo on his "good" day.

Blazes, he thought cheerfully, I'd certainly better be going fishing! Joe has to eat. He sat up, blinked till he was wide awake, and ran to poke his head out the door to answer Mr. Ek's question. "Yes!" he shouted back to him. "I am!"

"Had breakfast?"

"Get some in a jiffy. Had yours?"

"Yep." The little man attended to a fish on his line. "Bitin' like crazy this morning. Fall in the air, I guess. I'll drop back for you—say, thirty minutes?"

"Okay." Toivo wondered if his friend too had wakened with the thought that Joe's growing tummy was going to require fish, not milk, from now on.

He laid paper and kindling in the stove, opened the drafts, and struck a match; then quickly he brought water from the pail outside and poured some of it into the kettle. Now he added larger wood to the fire, set the teakettle forward, and partly closed the drafts. Soon bacon was sizzling in the pan; and its fragrance, combined with that of the wood pitch and the businesslike crackle of the flames, gave him for a moment his old secure feeling that all was well.

Things are set up for a while, anyway, he thought. He wondered if Joe was awake. That young guy had best be getting out of bed.

He's going to learn that fish come out of rivers and aren't caught in other people's boats, Toivo decided firmly, and when I finish these pancakes I'll go out and stir that little clown into action.

Soon he had added the dirty skillet to the one left from last night. He knew that he was going to have to do something about those sooner or later; but not this morning. Now—first, collect the fishing gear.

His pole, line, hooks, and lead sinkers soon were assembled.

Next, brush Joe and get off some of the mud from last night's raid. The young sea lion had to look his best for today's visit to the Rekkonens. Toivo went around to the box under the window, brush in hand, to be welcomed by Joe, as clean and glossy as he had ever been, for in drying, the mud had slipped neatly from his oily hide.

"Pretty soft." Toivo chuckled. "Built-in cleaning equipment." He shook the dust from the canvas after Joe had wriggled out of his bed, and dusted his hands with a flourish.

"Mr. Whiskers," he inquired with a bow, "how about a tom cod, sir, for your breakfast this morning?"

"*Ah-woohr,*" agreed Joe, willing to be reasonable but not quite taking in the full meaning of the offer, it seemed; for almost at once he began to "talk" about breakfast as though it had not just been mentioned. By weaving his neck from side to side, impatiently nudging

67

an old fish box, whiffing at a discarded net, poking his head in the door, and looking inquiringly about the house, he appeared to say, "Isn't there anything to eat? I'm asking you, Toivo, what do you intend to do about my breakfast?"

"You'll find out!" Toivo had heard Mr. Ek's oars as he came back for them.

"Your seal going to fish?" the little man asked as he slid his craft alongside; and Toivo winked an eye at him and shook his head.

"I don't think he knows that his breakfast is in the water. Shove off, Mr. Ek, without speaking to him, and let's see what he does." Toivo had taken his own place in the boat while saying this. Mr. Ek, looking somewhat puzzled, did as he'd been asked.

"No! *Ah-woohr!*" shrilled Joe, seeing the little boat pull away from the float. AH-WOOHR! I say 'AH-WHOO-OOHR!'" Right and left he slid along the edge of the platform, as he had done when Toivo first tried to get him to return to the water, and leaned far forward with his neck outstretched so that it seemed he must lose his balance, and the scolding "words" poured from him.

"Maybe this isn't going to work." Toivo frowned. "He can't understand why he is being treated that way and he's awfully hungry." He gave a whistle. And at that sound Joe almost instantly dived. After all, going in the direction of a whistle like that from Toivo had unfailingly resulted in a meal up until now. His dive was so satin-smooth and powerful that it made Mr. Ek catch his breath in admiration. And it carried the young seal deep and far. But when he surfaced he was close beside the boat.

68

"Ain't he somethin'!" Mr. Ek shook his head. "Will he follow along?"

"Yes. But I hope not too close, or he'll scare away his breakfast."

His hope was fulfilled. Joe stayed alongside only long enough to seem to be saying, "Well, I came, anyway," then dived again, for there were some things that he must do. The river bed must be checked; he needed to practice a few stunts he'd been working up—such as the one where he reversed direction while traveling in a circle at high speed—and, the one always sure to get a laugh from Toivo, the backward flip. And there was one other thing: he had seen a lot of good things to eat when he was under water a few minutes ago, the same kind of food he'd enjoyed when he had found it in that cross man's boat.

"He's done it!" cheered Toivo a little while later. "Look at the crazy galoot! He's caught a squid!"

"*Aw-hr -glp!*" remarked Joe, pleased with the food and the applause; and he swallowed his tidbit with a jerk and a twist of his face that was unmistakably play acting, then dived for more.

The next time he came up he held a small flounder in his teeth. Toivo and Mr. Ek gave him all the encouragement they could. From now on, Joe would at least help to provide for himself. Surely, Toivo thought, this would smooth his way somewhat with Hadge Jarvenin when he came home.

It was a good fish haul for all of them. Mr. Ek took a "nice string" home to his wife, and Toivo had enough for himself, and to make sure that Joe was provided for,

for a couple of days, even if the young seal himself had no luck during that time. The thing was to keep Joe's fish from spoiling. Sea lions did not eat cooked food. Toivo put some of the fish in a sack with a rock and let it down by a rope into the cold water under the float. Old Columbia would give the catch back to him in good condition in the morning. The rest of the fish he cut into bite-size pieces and one at a time fed them to Joe, discovering another of the young seal's talents; he was able to catch without fail anything tossed to him. Fish, of course, he preferred above all else.

"Joe," Toivo would call, ready to toss a bit, "fish, boy! Here!" And Joe caught. Throw to the right or to the left, throw higher or lower, or vary the rhythm of the tosses with a quick one, it made no difference. For a piece of fish Joe could open his mouth like a catcher's mitt, shift his stance sufficiently to insure his aim, and scoop in every bite.

"Hyvaa!" Toivo laughed aloud. "Good for you!" He would be sure that the Rekkonens saw this one! Then he realized that he was stuffing the little animal, and divided the remaining pieces of fish into two lots, one part to go into the skiff's box for Joe's lunch and the rest to be left at home for Joe's supper. Getting the fish ready was a dirty job and it took some time. The thought drifted half noted through his mind that he would be doing a good deal of this sort of thing from now on. He couldn't permit Joe to feed himself entirely from the river. He might wander too far, get into danger.

Now they were in the skiff and headed for the Rekkonen place. He would never forget this fine morning, Toivo thought, scanning the shore line appreciatively as

70

he pulled upstream. It was warm, but colored maples sifting bright leaves down onto the water spoke of an early fall. And the cottonwood trees spoke of it. They had turned their leaves to the silver side.

And they still surprise me, thought the boy, amused to recall that when he was younger he had tried to catch the silver leaves in the act of turning, but never been quick enough to observe the magic moment.

"It's a great time of year," he avowed to Joe, his passenger, who sat straight and watchful at the boat's stern; and Toivo felt the peace and sense of security he had learned to find in the sure return of the seasons.

River's chock-a-block with salmon, his thoughts ran on, seeing the silver fish leap from the water for whatever reason they had, and glimpsing schools of them beneath the surface of the water as they sped to upstream meeting places.

"There is one of the things nobody knows very much about, Joe: fish migration. Though I'll bet your grandpa could have explained it. Do you realize that those fish have been gone from here for three—maybe four—years? They've swum far and away, miles and miles away. Yet here they are back again, headed for the spot where they were hatched—to lay or to fertilize the eggs for their own young ones hatching."

"*Hwrr,*" remarked Joe, alert and listening. "You don't say."

"It's a fact. Scientists prove it. So what's the answer to that riddle? Do fish remember? Can they think? Does a salmon say 'Now I am going, and this is the way to the place?' " He looked at the twinkling eyes and whiskered face before him. "How is it done, Joe?" Joe tipped his head to the other side, but was silent.

"Aren't telling, huh?" Toivo's mind left the seasonal mystery of salmon, began to ponder more immediate questions.

"Hey, Joe," he inquired after pulling a hundred yards in silence, "what do you think the chances are that we'll have chicken for dinner? What'll you bet?" Joe was not a betting man. He ignored the question.

There probably would be chicken, the boy reflected. Mrs. Rekkonen, a Swedish lady, was a fine cook, and chicken was her specialty. She had a way of doing it that she claimed to have invented the first time she tried to cook with a Finnish cookbook and the results came out Swedish.

"In any nationality," said Toivo pulling a little harder on his oars, "chicken for me."

Olli and Selina were swimming when he sighted them, Olli just ready to dive. Their two dogs were romping, racing into the water and out again. Aarni was not there.

Finishing his chores, probably. When Mr. Rekkonen was away during the fish runs his family took care of the cows, pigs, chickens, and garden, as Toivo knew. Aarni, the oldest of the three children and already man size, could do a man's work.

"Hi!" yelled the two youngsters on the beach when they saw the skiff. "Here he comes! Toivo's coming!" They began to jump up and down and to shout for Aarni, and he came running from the barn. (Joe, amidst this excitement, slipped down onto the floor of the boat.)

"Got your seal, Toiv?" called Aarni, waving his long

arms, calling the dogs to him and holding their collars.
"Right here!"

"These fellas'll be okay." Aarni made his dogs sit, explained to them that they were not to bark. Toivo explained too to Joe that he need not be afraid; but Joe was not at all sure. There were no walls here or objects like grain barrels for him to hide between as there had been when he met Bingo at the barn that first time, Toivo thought the little sea lion might have been thinking. He slid the skiff onto the beach.

"Hello, everybody!" he called loudly. Funny, he always caught himself shouting here. That was the way you did at the Rekkonens. Everybody shouted. Now as they looked his way he saw all three pairs of blue eyes widen, heard his friends gasp in consternation; and spun around to see why.

Joe was leaving! His hind flippers were at the moment disappearing over the stern of the boat. The floundering young animal splashed into deep water, dived out of sight.

"Oh-h!" It was a united wail.

Aarni hurried over. "Toiv, this is—sure too bad!"

"He'll be all right." Toivo hoped he wasn't showing half the disappointment he felt.

"Will he—go home?"

"Probably will. Don't worry about it." (Toivo had decided then and there that he would leave as soon as he could and follow Joe.) "Only I wanted you all to see his tricks."

"Not tricks—already!"

"Yes." Toivo's eyes searched the water for sight of a small sleek head, scanned the river bank for a sight of hunters; but neither was visible. "You can hardly believe he knows so much."

"Aw," the children said, and stood around unhappily, not knowing what else to do. The dogs went to sit on the porch of the house, all the bounce taken out of them; and Mrs. Rekkonen looked out her door.

"Dis da happy holiday?" she asked, gazing in disapproval at dogs and children. "Not good." Then she bobbed her head and smiled at Toivo, and came to shake his hand in the stiff, polite old-country manner. "Ay'm glad to see our wisitor. Ve eat dinner at noon sharp, Toivo." And she chuckled mischievously, her blue eyes encircling her group and urging effort. "So—chicken, ya?" All her brood grinned back at her.

"Ya, Mamma!" they shouted. Then Toivo said his thanks, and everybody felt a bit more cheerful, he thought; but he wondered how long he could stand it, not knowing where Joe was.

"We should take a swim before dinner." Aarni had made an effort to speak brightly, and the others as always took their cue from him.

"Yeth." Selina touched Toivo's hand and began to run toward the water, "We better thwim!" Olli trotted out again onto the pier.

"Toiv, I can do the swan dive now!" yelled Olli.

"Go ahead!" Toivo made ready to swim. He had worn his swimming trunks next to his skin, and needed only to shed his outer clothes. He walked out onto the pier.

"Here goes!" Olli did the swan dive manfully, keeping his arms wide until the last moment before he hit the water—which everybody could see he was going to do with his stomach. They all cheered hard for him, however, and nobody said a word about his looking a little green in the face for a while afterward. You had to take a lot of punishment to learn the swan dive.

Toivo and Aarni dived together from the pier to race to a certain stick floating out there in the river, the last one back to be a sissy. "One, two, three—*go!*" Usually Aarni won these races. Today he didn't even have competition and swam the course alone, for Toivo met an interruption.

He had made a shallow dive, curving his arms and body to bring him quickly to the surface and get him on with the stroke; and, opening his eyes under water, could see Aarni's body not far away, curved in the same approved manner. But he could see another shape too! This was a swifter and more graceful shadow. He felt a nudge, and from below a determined force began to push him upward. His head broke the surface of the water a second before Aarni's head showed, but he did not go along with him to the bobbing stick. He stayed—to talk with Joe!

"Whiskered old fussbudget," he scolded him fondly. "Think you're smart, don't you?"

"*Aw-hoor,*" chuckled Joe, and did his backward flip. And all the kids came flocking.

With small talking sounds Joe said hello to all of them, and in an ecstasy at having so many admirers, splashed everybody with water and nudged all of them with his nose. The noise and shouting were so much more than even Mrs. Rekkonen was accustomed to that she again came out the door. Dusting flour from hands to apron, she ran down to look, and the two dogs padded after her but did not bark. Joe had favored them with a cold stare, and they stayed clear of him.

Olli found this hard to believe. "Mom," he shouted, "look. This critter's even got the dogs where he wants 'em!"

"What do you bet," puffed Toivo to Aarni, watching, "that this isn't just about the way it happened in the first place?"

"Huh?" Sometimes Toivo puzzled Aarni—always had.

"That's what Mr. Ek told me. He read someplace that millions of years ago seals used to be land animals."

"*Ei!*"

"He said something probably scared them into the ocean, and they just stayed there." Aarni was staring at him.

"*Millions* of years!"

"Sure. Wouldn't it take you that long"—Toivo was teasing now—"to turn your arms and legs into flippers?"

"Go on!" The bigger boy held out one of his own capable hands and shook his head at the idea of its ever being a flipper. Then he shouted, laughing, "Go on, now!" and slapped the hand flat down on the water to send a deluge over Toivo. "Race you!" he shouted again. This time Olli and Toivo and Joe all joined him in the rush to the goal. Aarni touched it first, but Joe had been there and back while he did that; and then the busy little sea lion dived down under all three of the boys, keeping a special eye on Toivo and nudging him back toward land.

"Just a worrywart." Toivo chuckled, secretly wishing that Joe were a little less bossy. Then another thought struck him. "Or maybe—well, I guess he's hungry. Anybody like to feed him?"

Everybody would; all of them wanted turns at feeding Joe. And they learned how to toss the pieces of fish Toivo had brought so that the sea pup could catch them. Joe insisted, however, upon staying in the water, where he sat tall and reached high, catching his meal as it was thrown to him from the pier. Clownish and silly, but always accurate in judgment, the little animal did not miss a single throw. When the fish was gone, Olli picked up his sister's large rubber ball.

"Throw that"—his older brother scowled at him— "and you'll go get it."

"I'll get it. Just want to see what the seal does when he can't open his mouth this big." Ollie tossed the ball to Joe in an easy curve, and the sea lion's neck stretched and his head came to meet the ball, but he did not open his mouth. He let the sphere hit his face as he gave a quick thrust upward, and thus sent it bouncing back again to Olli.

"Wow! Did you see him? Did you see that?" All the excited children yelled at one time, and Toivo, though less noisy, was as surprised as any of them.

"Wait a minute," Olli cried, "I'll try it up closer! I'll get down there where he is!" He retrieved the ball, took a position six or seven feet in front of Joe, with the two of them on the same level and both in the water. "Now —Joe!" Again Olli tossed the rubber ball, again and again; and each time, straight and sure, it came back to him. Mrs. Rekkonen, shaking her head, turned and started for her house.

"Mom, don't go away!" She only laughed and kept going.

"Ay better be cookin' dinner," she told the children. "Afraid dat animal begin doin' da polka or someting. Den Ay tink Ay gone crazy!"

Finally a rest was called. The children, not Joe, needed it. Toivo saw that Selina and the dogs were already on the beach when he turned to go in, and he hesitated, wondering what the opinionated Joe would decide to do about this.

What Joe did was to strike a compromise. He didn't go ashore but neither did he leave. He simply became stationary where he was. Sitting high, his back straight, looking like a tan and weathered piling, he waited close to the ledge that dropped off into deep water.

"He'll be okay there." Toivo came ashore, scooped a hollow in the sand for himself, and stretched out in it. "Days like this," he said to the others, "a fellow wishes summer could last forever."

"And you'd never grow up," nodded Aarni.

"Or go to school!" Olli too had made a hollow for himself, and now he moved in it restlessly. His little sister shook her head at him.

"I'm goin' to thkool. I'm big enough to read."

"No fooling?" Toivo gave one of her pigtails a pull. "Good luck then, Sis!"

"Thankth." Selina nodded with dignity.

There was silence for a while. The gulls wheeling as always overhead seemed not restless today, Toivo thought, but more content than usual. Lazily, water lapped against the pilings under the diving pier. Toivo dug his toes into the warm sand and wriggled down into his warm hollow. Soon he closed his eyes and dozed.

78

It was Mrs. Rekkonen's pounding on the triangle that awakened him. This was the call to dinner.

"Into clothes, everybody!" the Rekkonen kids shouted and scattered in various directions. Toivo looked again to make sure that Joe still waited, then made use of his skiff as a dressing room and hung his wet things on the gunwale to dry. His young seal watched. He surely would wait, the boy told himself, but felt uneasy.

As he walked up the beach toward the house he turned for one more look and raised his arm, making the all's-well signal with thumb and finger. The silent brown figure in the surf flipped over backward, but immediately was up again, big eyes watching.

"Race you to the house!" somebody shouted. It was Olli; and before the last word was out of his mouth he was off. Toivo and Aarni, thinking as one, immediately slipped their arms under Selina's elbows, ran with her swinging in the air between them, zoomed her, gasping and giggling, to a landing on the porch at the same instant that Olli arrived there. Olli glared.

"Sis beat!" shouted Aarni, glaring back at his younger brother.

Olli looked at the little girl's face: her round red cheeks and delighted blue eyes.

"Yeah," he said with a grin. "She sure did!"

It was a fried-chicken dinner, all right. With it Mrs. Rekkonen served hot biscuits and apple pie—and loud, happy conversation.

Imagine, Toivo said to himself as his eyes moved in wonder from face to face around that table, having it like this every day of your life. He felt that he must put this day deep in his memory, must always keep it.

Joe again sat willingly in the boat's stern on the way home. He had permitted Aarni to boost him there, and Aarni had said while he was doing this that he'd be down to see Toivo the next week sometime, that he had a special thing to tell him. Could they maybe do a little fishing?

You bet, they could. And this visit, Toivo reflected, would also be a good time to get Aarn's advice on what to do about his own problems. He hadn't wanted to bring them up today, hadn't wanted to remember them. You just couldn't announce right in the middle of a fine visit, he said to himself, watching the ripple of sunset gold on the water and the shadows purpling, that there is a chance you may be headed toward a foreign country before long and not come back. This "good" day was far better for not having had a thought like that in it. He tried, as he had done at the dinner table, to fill his eyes with the scene around him.

Always now I suppose shadows along the shore of any river in the world will look to me like evening on the Columbia. And green will be this green of the cottonwoods and their reflections. He felt not sad but peaceful; for somehow the happiness of the day was sustained in him.

"You have to believe things will come out for the best," he explained to Joe; and smoothly he slid his oars in and out of the water. Except for the cries of gulls overhead and the occasional splash of a salmon only the rivulets from the oar blades and the rhythmic friction of the rowlocks made any sound.

Toivo had boosted the young seal out of the skiff at the house door and made fast his boat before he glanced across and saw that his was not the only craft at moorage. Rising and falling with the movement of the water, silently waiting, was the *Gull.*

Silence was warning. Something was wrong—with his father!

SEVEN

Hadge was sitting at the table in the shadowed room and Toivo could not see his face clearly; but he appeared to be staring straight ahead of him at nothing. What had changed his plans? He'd sent that note last night by Mr. Rekkonen, saying that he was not to be expected for another week.

"Father?" Toivo came close. "I thought you weren't —" Then he saw Hadge's swollen hand lying like a red ham on the table and, on his forehead, the sweat of pain.

"Poisoning," whispered Hadge. "Cut, on a frozen fish."

"The doctor! Did you—"

"No!" The hurt man's voice struck like a blow. "No doctor. Costs too much." Then more quietly he ordered, "Do what I tell you."

"Sure. I will."

"Get ashes from the stove. Hot water. Soak this thing." Hadge bowed his head, holding back a groan; and Toivo hurried to follow directions.

Easy does it, he warned himself as he had done on that night when he found Joe. Don't panic, friend. He brought the round tub, set it on a chair near the swollen hand, put in the ashes and the hot water, and tested the temperature. Hadge lifted his hurt hand with his well one and let it sink deep in the hot time-tested mixture.

More water now, the boy ordered himself. Fill the kettle, the stove reservoir, the boiler. Routine was soon established: replace the cooling water in the tub with hot water; reheat this when it could be done, but bring in more water too and put it to heating; chop a supply of wood and bring it in; keep new wood on the fire; replace the cooling water in the tub . . .

Sometime during that night Toivo found time to whistle for Joe and to lay out for him the pieces of fish saved for his supper. Once he saw Joe looking through the window. During all this time Hadge did not speak again, but sank his arm and hand in the hot-ash mixture and swigged down the black coffee that Toivo had ready for him, while sweat poured from his face and body. If at any time he happened to notice either the shiny-clean room or the neatly made beds he gave no sign of it.

When morning came, Toivo blew out the lamp and his father lifted a haggard but relieved face. They had saved the arm, Hadge said. The red lines and swelling were less noticeable and the pain was much better. It would be safe to sleep for a while.

Toivo did not care to sleep. He opened the door and leaned there, taking deep, grateful breaths of morning air; and it seemed to him a long time since yesterday, his "good day." It seemed a long time since he had been a little boy, when there were plenty of good days.

"What happens now?" asked the boy of the river and the sky, lifting his face to them. "What now?"

The answer to that question of Toivo's soon became clear. Hadge must stay at home. He could not work for a long time, because the fish poisoning had undermined his strength and left his right hand stiff. This was bitter knowledge for the big man, hard for him to accept. He sat in his chair for many days, his thin hands lying listlessly in his lap, after being told by his friends that this was the truth.

For his son such despair was frightening to watch, for he was experiencing for the first time in his life the absence of his father's strong hold upon his own well being. It was no less frightening because of his realization that unless he himself could somehow earn enough money the Jarvenins were not going to be able to meet their expenses. In addition, there was Joe, here in spite of Hadge's wishes. Joe must be kept from worrying him.

"The thing for you to do," the Eks and the Rekkonens constantly told the discouraged man, "is to move those stiff fingers of yours—exercise the wrist. You will work again. And you will carve with the wood." One day Hadge began to respond. After that Toivo watched him clenching and unclenching his hand, progressing a little each day as the weeks crept by.

"The money I wanted to earn—the trap springer," Hadge would say fiercely, "even your education—may have to wait. But these hands—I will have!" He forced himself to pick up his cup or a dish—or his carving knife. And often he would quote the Finnish proverb hopefully—that "The son, wiser than the father, will put by a nest egg for his future."

"He's getting better," reported Toivo to everyone. And when October ended, he said, "He's going to be all right." Then, frowning in dismay at his own thought and the feeling of relief it brought him, he would add to himself, we won't be leaving here, now. Not for a long time.

Almost guiltily every morning, because of this feeling of relief, he would put breakfast on the table for his father and himself and cut up some fish for Joe. He kept wondering why Hadge did not remark upon Joe's presence there and what he would say when he did finally mention it; he was torn between his need for the love and companionship of his pet and the desire to let his father know that the bond between them as father and son was as strong as ever.

From now on, he decided, he must give all his earnings to Hadge to buy food. And as soon as he could he would hunt for work that paid more than did his chores for Mr. Ek. With this change in mind, he worked hard to get things in shape at the farm so that Mr. Ek could spare him.

"I'll be late getting home today," he said to Hadge one morning, ready to leave for the barn. "Going to clean out the vegetable patch, do some spading so the rains will drive in the fertilizer."

"The famous Oregon rains." Hadge shivered, speaking somberly in his native tongue and looking as bleak as the weather ahead of him. "Somebody finds them good?"

"Sure! Rain puts all the missing elements right back into the earth." Toivo had made his statement as though with knowledge few could possess, and his father lifted a wry eyebrow.

"So? Sounds reasonable." He drained his coffee cup.

"Others, I hear, have arrived at a similar conclusion." A bit red in the face, Toivo filled the cup, then was called to the door.

"Aarni!" he shouted when he saw who was there. "Get in here!" This visit, promised before Hadge's accident and then postponed, he now happily welcomed. But as he ushered his friend into the room his feeling turned to disappointment. "Blazes. I have to work all day."

"Yeah. Uncle Sam told me." The tall visitor eased into a chair. "How about takin' me on as a hand? We'd have time to fish then."

"Wow!"

"Coffee?" Hadge pushed forward another cup and Toivo filled it for Aarni. "Not bad. And besides, from what I am told, you are going to need all the help you can get today."

Toivo laughed aloud. "Father is making fun of me. I got carried away by my great knowledge of farming. We are doing some extra chores over there, though." Suddenly his heart felt lighter than it had been for some time, for he and his father were joking again. Big Hadge Jarvenin not only was better; he felt better toward his son, and had forgiven him for talking back that day.

"Don't you have enough work of your own to do," he said with a grin to Aarni, "without helping do mine?"

The tall boy set down his cup. "Wanted to tell you about that," he said quietly—so quietly that for a while Toivo failed to perceive that this was an important announcement. "Olli is doin' the work at home, now, because I've got me a job." Toivo glanced up and saw the glow on the speaker's face and suddenly realized what had been said. He was ready to burst with pride for Aarni.

"Why, you big crazy galoot!" He jumped up and began to pound his friend on the back. "A job! You aren't old enough! Where are you working?"

"On the *Sue Elmore*. She's a little freighter that runs along the coast. Beginning tomorrow, I'll be a deck hand on her."

"The steamer to Tillamook. Carries a few passengers too. I know her!"

"What is she like?" asked Hadge. "Special build, they say."

"Her keel is made special. It's a big, twenty-four-inch-square beam, to take her over the bumps into Tillamook Bay."

"Whopping big beam," marveled Toivo.

"All the way through she's like that—extra good. I'm hopin' her cook is good too!"

What a fellow Aarni was! Toivo looked at him and felt himself very young and foolish. Why couldn't he— With stunning impact the thought struck him: perhaps he could! He leaned forward to speak his thought, but it must already have been written on his face, for Aarni, with a quick glance at Hadge, who was putting sugar in his coffee at the moment, murmured a warning.

"Hold it, Toiv," and after a moment added, "they took me for older than I am."

"Did?" Toivo let his thought die. He stood up to leave for the barn and Aarni jumped to go with him. Both boys noticed as they stepped outside that Hadge had reached for his knife and some scraps of alder and cottonwood.

"That will help make the day go by for him," said Toivo with a nod.

"He's a real artist, Toiv." Aarni shook his head. "All those little wooden figures."

"Well," said little Mr. Ek when the two boys and accompanying sea lion reported for work, "let's all stay together as we go, instead of separating with the chores. More fun that way."

"I'd like to put the seal through that milking stunt everybody talks about," Aarni told him. "Could we divide up enough so's I get that part?"

"It's yours," Mr. Ek and Toivo agreed. And Toivo pointed to Bingo and Yellow One streaking from the house today without waiting for a whistle, and to Joe, who was meeting those two with an excited weaving of his body and a stream of "talking" sounds. "Try and keep up with them!"

"I see what you mean!" Aarni had jumped and stood astride to let the pets rush between his legs. "They always like this?" he yelled, running after them toward the barn.

Holding back laughter until it threatened to choke him, Aarni had grabbed a pail and milking stool, the others saw when they came in, and was sitting down to milk the first cow, beside which the cat, the dog, and the sea lion already were waiting. Blue eyes teasing, he kept them waiting for a short moment, and they watched him, intent and hopeful.

When the moment grew too long, nervous tongues began to lick little noses, and Joe's flippers beat the floor; then the practiced milker's hands went to work.

Steadily, in the rhythm that only practice can produce, the warm streams struck the pail, and in a moment one stream arched through the air toward Bingo. The little dog was ready, with mouth wide open, and took the milk down inside him with gulps of delight. The cat took her turn; some of the milk stream reached her thirsty throat, but more of it soaked her threshing paws and festooned her chin. Sea lion Joe had his turn. And easily, neatly, he snuffled that entire stream into his big mouth without waste. Toivo could hear Aarni's breath being drawn deeply. He went through the stunt over and over again, trying to catch one of the three animals off guard and surprise it, but this couldn't be done. Always they were ready for him.

Toivo and Mr. Ek moved on down the barn, filling grain boxes, forking hay down from the loft; and Mr. Ek sang in his always surprisingly big voice while he worked. His song, "Over the Bounding Main," suited the swinging rhythm of his hayfork, and the two boys in good spirits began to sing along with him:

"Sailing, sailing, over the bounding main!
Many a stormy wind shall blow
Ere Jack comes home again."

The way they sang it, the old song rolled and dipped like the sea. It bellowed and blew; and Aarni, standing up to lift aside a pail of milk, sang loudest of all, not missing a beat, even when he stopped moving and stared at the sea lion. He stared but kept on singing, afraid that Joe might stop what he was doing, trying to get a message to his uncle and to Toivo to tell them about it.

"Sailing, Joe-oe. For gosh sakes', look at Joe-oe," he chanted, eyes fastened on the sight.

"Sailing—*look, look*—over the bounding main!" Then the others saw what was going on. Joe was cavorting. He was balance-and-bowing, whirling and dipping to the music of the sailing song. It wasn't like the other time, Toivo told himself excitedly, when Joe had bobbed his head as though to beat a rhythm with the gramophone: this time he was *dancing!* Very carefully, the boy stepped out into the barn arena. Smoothly and slowly, so as not to startle Joe, he too began to step and whirl with the singing. In a moment Mr. Ek, then Aarni, had joined him. Round and round then, in hilarious song and dance, man and boys and strange little beast, all of them whirled, until the human beings were exhausted and threw themselves, red in the face and gasping, down onto the hay to rest. Joe, quite as full of ginger as before his exercise, looked down his nose at them.

"*Aw-hwr,*" remarked Joe. "Poor weak things."

"What I'd like to know," exploded Aarni, sitting up when he had caught his breath and glaring at Toivo, "is how in thunder you're ever going to get up the nerve to put a critter like that back into the ocean?" His uncle frowned and shook his head at him. No one, Mr. Ek seemed to be trying to tell Aarni, ever brought up this subject. Time enough when Toivo had to face it. However, since it *had* been brought up . . .

"What else," he demanded of his nephew, "can a fellow do? Sounds like you don't know much about the size of a grown he-sea lion."

"Pretty big?"

"Ten feet high, thereabouts. Weigh fifteen hundred, two thousand pounds."

Aarni stared. Uncomfortably he glanced at Toivo and stood up. "Time to get to work, I guess."

"You're welcome to put Joe in the old shed if you want," offered Mr. Ek after dinner when the boys were stopping work to go fishing. "It's cool for him in there, and there's a catch on the door." He gave a little chuckle. "Of course you may come back and find him dancing again—this time to his own singing. But if that happens, we are all in it together, and we can promise to tell the world none of us is a lunatic."

"Sounds okay." Toivo felt relieved. He had been wondering what would be the best way to leave Joe for a while. "We'll be going too far to have him swim alongside and we don't want him in the boat, gobbling our catch. I'll leave him in the shed, then take him for a swim and make it up to him after I get home."

Joe scolded a little, mildly at first, when the boys cleared a place for him in the little building, and looked at Toivo as though puzzled by his poor manners. Strange way to treat your best friend, the young seal appeared to be thinking. Especially when that friend can do flips— and throw a ball—and dance.

Even when the shed door was locked he seemed more annoyed than concerned; but as the skiff moved downstream the boys heard his voice rising, registering disappointment.

"*Aw-woohr!* [Where you going?]" wailed Joe.

Toivo frowned uneasily. "He knows every squeak of

this boat, and right now he's hearing all of them. It was his first friendly port."

"We don't have to go. Still want to?"

"Sure. He's perfectly all right. He's not always going to be able to go everywhere I do. Besides, this is about our last chance for a trip before winter sets in."

They took turns with the oars and before long they had passed Tongue Point and the cove was out of sight. They let the river carry them and dragged their lines.

"Bet you're excited, Aarn," began Toivo, "being on your own."

"Get to thinkin' about it," admitted the big boy, "and sometimes I don't hear Ma and Pa speakin' to me."

"Guess you will miss everybody a little."

"Yeah." Aarni dragged one hand in the water. "S'pose people get over it, though."

"Some do," observed Toivo. "Some don't." He leaned forward eagerly. "What's the first thing you are going to buy with your money?"

"*Buy!*"

"Why, yes. Don't you want something—very much?"

"I want my own piece of land. I want a good, rightly managed farm that'll make your mouth water."

"No more school?"

"Toiv, you should know—I'm not much of a student."

"I'm not so sure of that. But I hope you get whatever you want most."

"Now you; you like school. Always come out on top of the class and all that."

"I'd go without anything and everything to get to school this winter. It takes a long time to learn to be a doctor." Toivo, who was rowing, shipped his oars

92

and let the skiff drift once more. "I didn't tell you, but before his accident my father was all for leaving the country right away and going back to Finland. Now— I don't know what's happened to that wild idea, but I think he still intends to go when he can."

"You got to be foolin'!"

"Nope."

"You—you'd be a foreigner!"

"One way or another, I would."

"Maybe now your pa—" Aarni was interrupted by the sound of gunfire, and glanced shoreward, scowling. "Been a lot of that lately!"

"The paid seal hunters, and anyone else who takes a notion." Toivo's voice grew tight, angry. "It's great sport. You have a moving target, a big one—and what's the difference if something living is left to die slowly? Nothing but an animal. It can't tell on you!"

"Sometimes," murmured Aarni, his blue gaze on the horizon where soon his own world would open for him, "you get discouraged about people. All those millions of years you were talkin' about—don't seem to have changed *us* much."

At sundown the boys returned to the houseboat. It was too late, Aarni said, for him to stop for a swim; and he stepped into his own boat to hurry along home.

"Be seein' you!" he called.

"Stop by every time you can!" Toivo walked toward Mr. Ek's place to get Joe. They would take a swim, to cheer old Joe. Then he'd cook supper. He was near the shed when he glanced up—*saw the smashed shed door* —and began to run!

EIGHT

Toivo stumbled, shouting as he ran.

"Joe!" he called. "Here, boy! Where are you?" No sound came in reply, and only the hole in the splintered door looked back at him from the shed.

He dropped to his knees, crawled through the opening, and searched the interior of the small building. Signs of the young seal's restlessness were everywhere: an overturned oil can sent rolling and its contents spilled, a stack of old stovepipes crashed to the ground, the light sleigh in which Mr. and Mrs. Ek sometimes rode to church pushed against the wall. The dirt floor too was scraped and scarred from the countless turnings of a heavy, restless body.

"Joe!" shouted Toivo again as he crawled outside and looked up and down the yard, his voice cracking in spite of himself because the signs of the seal's worry and unhappiness were plain to read and because there were echoing in his mind sounds he'd been hearing all afternoon, sounds of gunshot.

Now Mr. Ek was running toward him from the house, calling something. "Take it easy, boy!"

"How long has he been gone?"

"Must have broke out early, though nobody heard any

of it. Your pa said to me to take the motorboat, and I've been up and down, but nobody I asked has seen Joe. Follerin' you, do you think?"

"Maybe not." Toivo glanced at the sky and the river shadows and estimated the time of day. Another half hour of daylight. "If he's hurt," he said, forcing his voice into evenness, "then he could be caught under the floats. Suction's strong under there."

"Let's look." Mr. Ek turned at once, buttoning his jacket as he ran in the direction of the houseboat.

There had been nothing under there. The whirling eddies about the pilings and the green half light beneath the rotting planks of the floats gave no clue of Joe. Neither did the darkening surface of the river reveal him; though Toivo, making one last try in his skiff, imagined troubled eyes in every shadow.

Finally, forced to drop the search, Toivo made fast his boat and his feet dragged him home. Hadge's glance lifted to meet his as he came in through the doorway.

"I am sorry," the quiet man said; and Toivo nodded, as wooden as the carving in his father's hand. "The sea pup means much to you."

"Thanks for having Mr. Ek pass the word along the river." The boy hung up his jacket, put fuel on the fire, kept his voice carefully level, and said the polite words he thought he should be saying to his father. "Glad to see you carving again."

Hadge laid his work aside. "Sit here," he said. Toivo dropped into the chair pushed toward him. Hadge appeared to be selecting words.

"Your pet grows large," he finally began.

"Pretty large."

"Now, at eight or nine months of age his weight is almost as much as your own. Do you know how large he will grow?"

Toivo frowned. "I have heard—people say he may weigh—a ton."

"And this huge one—must have fish to eat. He will go hunting for them, is this not so? And meet the hunters?"

"Don't worry about that! I'll keep him fed, all right, here at home. If I can just—get him back again—safe."

"Always, Toivo? To fish for him? To stay close to him?"

"I'll fix a place where I can leave him when I have to."

"Like now, eh? Today?"

"*No!*" The driven boy jumped to his feet. "No, I'll fix something!" He pulled his voice down once more. "You have to give Joe credit, Father. He tries—hard—to please us."

"That is true." Hadge looked at his son a long moment, unspoken thoughts in his eyes.

"What are you thinking to yourself?"

"That if we cannot find your pet now, you must understand this had to happen—and it is neither your fault nor the seal's."

"But not like this! With winter close." Tears did sting Toivo's eyes now. "Not with him thinking I didn't want him—that I'd gone off and left him!"

"I think," said Hadge, "that he does not misunderstand you."

"Thanks." Toivo would have gone outside again to escape further talk; but his father had one more thing to say.

"In case your seal is found, boy"—the words were firm—"he must this time go back to the sea."

"But he'd miss us! He almost thinks he is a person!"

"Nature will tell him—the truth."

"I think you believe"—Toivo studied his father's face, his own face pale—"that he may have left us this afternoon to swim out to sea, but that most probably—he is dead."

"I believe that you must be prepared—never to know."

Tiredly, Toivo prepared food, cleared up after it, crept beneath his blankets. He turned his back to the empty window and lay for a long time wide-eyed. At last he fell asleep. But when early morning began to lighten the river he was awakened by the sound of scratching close by, and jumped from his bed to look outside.

Underneath the window, unable to get into his box or to lift himself to look in at Toivo because of his wounds, huddled Joe! Hadge wakened and lit the lamp as Toivo ran out onto the deck; then between them they carried the wounded young sea lion into the house.

Joe's tan coat was drenched with his red blood. The injury was long, a furrow down his right side from shoulder to hip; but the bullet had not penetrated his body, and they thought he would live.

They bandaged him with strips of cloth wound round about; and their young patient was too weak to object.

November passed slowly, with Toivo oppressed by the knowledge that even if Joe got well, time had run out for him to live safely as a pet. His father had been right.

It's plain enough, the boy told himself, trying to look

97

squarely at the issue. Either he stays with me and is shot again—or we put him out in the ocean. It's a great choice. And I wish somebody would help me make it. Each day, each night, as the hours saw the sea youngster closer to recovery from his mishap, Toivo felt might be his last with Joe.

By the time Aarni came by the house on his next day off, the young seal was no longer an invalid; he had only a stripe of white hair growing along the scar down his side to remind anyone of his injury. Not only was young Joe's wound healed, but, it seemed to Toivo, his strength and his devotion to lifeguard duty when they were in the water had increased tenfold.

People in swimming, the sea lion always seemed to be thinking, need help from an expert like me. Always he would flash beneath Toivo when the boy made a dive, hustle down into the water beneath him, and determinedly push him up to the surface.

"You think you're pretty big!" Half exasperated, Toivo would scramble to the float after being pushed within reach of it and snug into his jacket. "Mister, in this cold—I didn't want to swim anyway!" Joe didn't guess that he was the reason they were both out in the winter chill and that Toivo was on guard to keep his pet safe.

"*Aw-hoowr!*" Joe would have scoffed unbelievingly. He loved the winter. His extra layer of fat served well as an overcoat.

"You're never cold. Probably be warm as toast—out there in the ocean or even on an iceberg." Toivo sometimes asked the seal the direct question. "Could you make out all right, Joe?" He would tip the funny whiskered face upward and look into the wise big eyes. "Think you'd be lonesome?"

"Let me take Joe out over the bar for you next time we sail," Aarni suggested to Toivo and Hadge when he came by one day in December. "Little guy knows me and wouldn't be afraid. I've already told the men a lot about him. Captain will let us put him off real easy, once we're outside."

"Just dump him out there and leave him?" Toivo paced restlessly in the little room. "Seems such a low-down trick."

"Low-down trick is when animals are left without their knowing how to get food or find friends! A sea lion knows right where his food is. And they all seem to club together. Besides—the ocean's where Joe comes from."

"He may not remember that."

"Old Ma Nature, she'll remember."

"That's what Father thinks. But it's hard to—" Toivo walked over to look out the window at Joe, asleep now on the deck because his box was beginning to crowd him. They could make a bigger box, the boy said to himself; they could probably find bigger and bigger places for him, but then . . . He looked at the scar down Joe's side, recalling the bullet wound and the young animal's warm blood streaming from him, his life almost gone, and drew a long breath.

"All right," he said, whirling around to face his father and Aarni. "Help me, will you?"

They helped him. Hadge put aside his carving and built a crate to carry Joe. One side and the top of the crate were of coarse wire mesh so that there would be as little as possible of a shut-in feeling for the young sea lion; and there was a door that could be easily removed when the moment came from Joe to slip into the ocean.

"Seems as if there would be a better time for this than the middle of winter," fumed Toivo, nailing to the floor of the crate the piece of canvas on which Joe had been sleeping.

"Best time, middle of winter," Aarni declared. "I've been askin' all around. Everybody says this is the time when sea lions are settling down to stay in one place for a while. There will be some on the rocks all along the coast until spring." He had returned from home with his father's small wood scow and some strong line, and now—with Joe in the crate—began to lash this firmly to the scow. Hadge would take the scow in tow with his motorboat. "Joe's goin' to do all right," said Aarni.

"You believe that?"

"The others get along. And this one's smart!"

"I know." In his mind Toivo began to go over the various things he and Joe had done that day.

They had had Joe's swim early, earlier than usual because the youngster was in high spirits and needed a workout. Watching him romp with no idea of what was to happen to him, Toivo had felt an almost unbearable sense of loss. Not only was he losing Joe and all that the happy young animal's trust and comradeship had meant to him, but much else. He was losing his last hold on childhood. How he had wished that it was summer again and that he could take his pet and go up to the Rekkonens for a romp with the kids, wished it were the summer just gone, with its lazy afternoons, the garden ripening in the sun, and old Aarni the crazy boy he had been, instead of the tired, grown-up deck hand he had become.

After the swimming, he recalled, he had brushed Joe —brushed the wiry outer hair and the soft under hair, seeing that all the baby coat of brown was gone now and the light tan coat established, a tan lighter than that of the average Steller seal. He had observed too that the scar down the young sea lion's side made a ridge under the brush, and had realized that the streak of white hair growing along the scar would always be there. Joe had held still for the brushing, but this was not easy for him to do.

Then Toivo had said to him, "Dinner, Joe—catch!" and the gay young fish eater had instantly backed off, been ready. Tail-end swaying and supple neck weaving, eyes alert, he had been ready with his catcher's-mitt mouth to scoop from the air every piece of fish thrown to him. When there was no more fish, Toivo remembered, and he had shown his empty hands, Joe had put on an act of despair, making a silly woebegone face, then falling backward.

"Yes. You're so right. This one, Aarn, is smart."

The whirl of water around Tongue Point made a moment of trouble for the lightweight scow when they went down river on Aarni's next free day, and Toivo was torn with pity for Joe as a jerk on the tow line threw the young seal onto his side and hard against the side of the crate; but once this spot was safely passed, the journey to Astoria was uneventful, merely long and cold. They came at last in sight of the *Sue Elmore*.

Since high water was always in the ship's favor she was hustling her loading when they saw her. The ship's boom, with the help of a winch and giant hooks, was picking up freight from the docks, lowering it onto the deck or into the hold, where deck hands with their carts stowed it in its proper places. The *Sue Elmore* had steam well up, Toivo noticed. Two or three of the men waved to Aarni, and after a few minutes the captain called down to him.

"We'll take y'r seal aboard in the net, Aarn!" He gestured with one thumb over his shoulder. "Run y'r craft 'longside the dock. The boys'll hoist 'im!"

"Ay, sir." The responsibility brought drops of perspiration to Aarni's upper lip, but his actions were calm. "Head over there, will you, Mr. Jarvenin?" He gestured toward an enormous net now being spread on the dock. Several men jumped to lift Joe and his crate to the center of this net when the *Gull* was alongside, and now the corners of the net were drawn together by ropes. It was picked up by the loading hook and hoisted on a line from the boom.

Joe had been trusting until the crate swung out over space and he felt himself swaying with the net, then his head lifted anxiously, and he turned his eyes toward Toivo. The watching boy had all he could do to keep from calling out that everything would be all right and not to worry. Then the crate came to rest on the forward deck. He could no longer see the way Joe looked.

"That's the works!" sang out the loaders, and the captain signaled that the *Sue Elmore* was ready to sail.

"The reason Joe's where he is," explained Aarni of the placing of the crate, "is so he'll be quick to slip out and into the water, once we reach a smooth stretch. With the crate held low in the water, he'll skedaddle out the little door and be free in no time."

"Oh, sure." Toivo's voice was so rough, as he pulled a piece of tarp across his shoulders and half over his face, that both companions glanced at him. "Let's get going!"

They settled into the trip home. Hadge spun the engine and put about, headed the *Gull* upstream. There was a dull December mist hanging over the water, and they hunched their backs against the cold. No one glanced back. No one cared for conversation.

After a while, remembering that his father had put in a hard day and must be very tired, Toivo nodded to him to exchange places, and took over the navigation of the boat. No one spoke until the *Gull* had rounded the point at the Eks' place. Then Aarni had a question.

"What do you suppose Aunt Elin's so steamed up about?"

Big Mrs. Ek with a shawl over her head and clutched about her shoulders, the others saw, was hurrying across the runway to meet them.

NINE

Through the mist as the *Gull* chugged in for her moorage, Toivo could see Mrs. Ek waiting on the float. Her manner told him that the good lady thought she had brought fine news for someone. Probably she had some mail for Hadge. He failed to care greatly for the time being, however, what Mrs. Ek had to say. All Toivo wanted at this moment was to be alone to convince himself all over again that the best thing possible had been done for Joe. Quietly, while Hadge and the others talked, he slipped toward the house door.

In a vague way he was aware of the grayness around him and knew that snowflakes had begun to fall; but the grayness seemed part of himself, and he did not feel the flakes melting on his face or see them clinging wetly to the pile of old fish net beside the runway and to Joe's box beneath the window. Through his threadbare jacket he felt the cold, however, and shivered.

Where do sea lions go, he wondered, in weather like this? Where will you sleep, Mr. Whiskers? His hand had reached the doorknob when Aarni's voice stopped him.

"Hey, Toiv! Message from a friend of yours!"

"Yes!" Mrs. Ek explained brightly, as if she helped. "Eb Parhaneimi!" The long name had rolled thumpingly from her tongue as though she were used to saying it, but Toivo didn't know what she was talking about. That person was a stranger to him. He sighed. All too evidently this was to be one of Mrs. Ek's well-meant cheering-up programs; and today he had no wish for it. He was about to nod and turn away again.

Aarni laughed. "Look at old Toiv blink his eyes at what you said, Aunt Elin."

"*Ei!*" The big lady chuckled. "I did it again. Toivo, I should have said Eb Smith. The doctor—my cousin." She pulled her shawl more tightly about her. "He is coming here for Christmas. That's what I wanted to tell you."

"Oh. Yes. Doctor Smith." Toivo knew he was sounding foolish. Aarni came to his rescue with an explanation of his aunt's slip of the tongue.

"Cousin Eb changed his name to Smith a long time ago. The family's never got used to it." Toivo only half listened.

One word out of all those that had just been said was echoing in his tired mind, and he blinked with the surprise of it.

"Christmas," he said. He turned to Aarni. "It's almost here."

"What's the trouble?" The tall boy cocked a questioning eye. "Screw loose somewhere?"

"I guess—I must have." How could he, how could anyone, he wondered, let the holiday come so close without thought of it? Why, always—at home and at school, there had been plans and celebrating— Then his mind began to function. "Well, blazes, if Doctor Smith is coming, he must have come in on the *Sue Elmore!*

Why didn't we bring him back with us?" Aarni nodded in mock solemnity.

"Guess you'll hold together," he decided.

Mrs. Ek smiled. "Eb'll be out later, on the train from Astoria. Being as he's Father Christmas for the party, he has some shopping to do." She turned to Hadge. "Mr. Jarvenin, we are having an old-country celebration, the first we've held in this neighborhood. And you and Toivo are especially invited. There will be dinner at noon on the twenty-fourth, and on Christmas morning early the race to church service at the school, provided there's snow enough for sleighs. Do come." Hadge bowed his thanks; then he and Toivo went into the house together. Tiredly, Toivo dropped into a chair.

Would he sometime feel again, he wondered, the old happy excitement about Christmas, or had he lost it? Did you lose the ability to be happy? When you had been through a thing like this with Joe—knew you had tricked a friend— Joe had trusted him.

Hadge, striking a match to start a fire, sent a glance his way. "Rough day," he said.

"Mm."

"Remember—your seal is better off."

"Did it seem to you that he was—afraid?"

"I did not think so."

"Of course he thought all the time—until he swung out over our heads—that I was going along with him."

Hadge had no reply.

They sat for a while, the two of them. The gray light of the December afternoon lay against the windows, and now and then a snowflake fluttered on the pane. The fire burned quietly.

The ground was white when Toivo looked out in the morning, and the snow still fell—without wind, straight down. The river, swollen and full of debris to which the snow had clung, was an ugly color. Sea gulls rode the brush fragments as they careened downstream, using these for take offs and resting places while they fished. When Toivo came into the house with wood for the wood box he found that Hadge, for the first time since his accident, had the fire going and was cooking breakfast.

"Feeling better, Father?"

"Invalid days are over." Hadge flexed his fingers, no longer stiff. "When the work comes, I'm ready for it. Beside, I'm thinking that you should begin early today, boy, to take care of those cows and horses of yours. Snow is hard on them."

"You're right." Toivo took his own coffee to the window to drink it while looking out. "They can't go out to pasture, that's sure." He thought of the comfortable warmth of the barn with the wood stove heating water in the shop down at the far end and of the good smell of hay and fresh milk, and pictured Bingo and Yellow One racing to meet Joe—who would not be there. It seemed to him that never again could he go to the barn. Suddenly, however, he recalled that Doctor Smith was now over at the Eks' house, and that he could answer some questions about the winter habits of sea lions. Toivo hurried to get ready.

"You will need to change into dry shoes," Hadge told him soberly. "Both pairs of yours have holes in them."

"That's okay. I'll change." Toivo buttoned his jacket, pulled down his cap, picked up the extra shoes. He had no gloves, but he would not be out-of-doors very long, anyway. At the door he turned back to ask a question. "You—going to that Christmas party?"

"To stay away would be discourteous."

"We don't have presents to take."

"That they knew when they invited us." Toivo nodded, closed the door, and had started across the walk when he heard the Rekkonens coming down river. Apparently they were having no trouble; they sounded cheerful as always. Their shouting carried pleasantly to him, lifted his spirits. He ran to shore and was ready to help make fast their boat when they came in. Both the brothers were rowing, he could see as they came. Their mother and sister were with them. Mr. Rekkonen was probably already down here at his sister's house helping with preparations.

"Had to come early!" the occupants of the Rekkonen boat informed Toivo as they stepped ashore sparkling and gay in colored caps, scarves, and mittens, each one carrying a basket or box. "Had to bring some of the decorations and things to finish down here. Aunt Elin is going to make us get everything—even the visit to the sauna—done before noon!"

"Sauna!" Toivo shivered extravagantly. "Not with *snow!*"

"Absolutely. That's the way they did it!"

"Want to help get this plunder squared away?" Aarni asked. "Then we can go along with you and lend a hand at the barn."

"Sure thing." Toivo picked up all the luggage he could carry; and arriving at the house with it had time for a few minutes with the man he so much admired,

Doctor Smith, who already had been told of Joe's banishment.

"That wasn't an easy thing for you, Toivo."

"Joe is—somebody to know."

"A real fellow." The doctor shook his head. "A personality like that in an animal—affectionate, loyal, humorous—makes a man wonder just how far his own kind may have come—and has yet to go."

"How do you mean?"

"Oh, we bumble along, most of us, so unknowing. We don't see or hear or understand a miracle in nature, like Joe."

He knows how I feel, and he can put it into words. That was Toivo's thought. And he knew now more surely than ever that to be a doctor, a man of science and wisdom, was his big ambition.

"They say," added the doctor as an afterthought, "that there's a wild-life refuge over on the coast not far from where I live."

"Do you think Joe might head for that?"

"Does seem likely."

Toivo ran to the barn, the cat and dog racing ahead of him, Olli and Aarni close at his heels, and began to work and to try to keep his thoughts on what must be done. The other boys, he soon began to realize, were making an effort to lighten his task for him.

At those times when he turned to glance over his shoulder as though Joe were there, or waited out of habit for the lolloping young creature to catch up with him, and then brought himself back to the reality of his pet's absence, one or the other of the young Rekkonens would burst in on his thoughts with some antic to distract him. After a time that seemed not nearly as long as he had thought it would be the hour came for going to the house. There, before they came in, they met their first hint of the celebration.

"RAUHALLISTA LOULUA!" A hand-printed greeting on a large poster welcomed them when they came puffing up onto the porch. "GOD JULE!" hailed another sign on the wall of the good-smelling kitchen when they had stamped the snow from their boots and come inside.

"Both the signs say 'Merry Christmas,' don't they?" Tovio asked.

"Yep!" Olli shouted his answer laughingly. "Once for the Finns, and once for the Swedes, including Mom."

"On account of she'th a Thwede," explained Selina.

"Well! There is a lot to do before noon!" Mr. Ek reminded everyone. "Fire's been burnin' all night at the sauna. We'd best get goin' out there."

"Men first?" shouted Aarni.

"Yep. While the ladies start the cookin'."

"Then what are we waitin' for?" The brothers raced away toward the shed at the side of the house, and Toivo and his father, Sam Ek, Aab Rekkonen, and Doctor Smith, with varying degrees of eagerness, followed after them.

In this shed large rocks under which fires had been burning were very hot. When water was poured over them, causing billows of thick, penetrating steam to roll through the room, the men and boys lay in the blankets of steam, moving their arms and legs and slapping themselves all over with little bundles of birch switches to stir up lively circulation.

Soon Toivo's body was bright red from toes to hair-line. The steam grew hotter and hotter, until the moment when he felt he could endure it no longer; then a signal was given and everyone burst out the back door into the cold air. Everyone threw himself down into the snow!

"Roll!" Aarni shouted to Toivo, his bowl-cut hair slapping his face as he followed his own advice. "Roll hard! It feels good!"

It did feel good too. Toivo was surprised. Though gasping for breath at contact with the cold, he felt no inner chill, but a warmth in his blood—a great exhilaration! He rolled and rolled in the snow; while Hadge nearby, sounding more alive and closer to laughter than he had been in a long time, rolled as the others did.

"Now! Quick!" Sam Ek gave the order, and everybody jumped up and ran again, this time to a small dressing room beyond a partition; and here each one dressed in a completely clean outfit. Now, full of good will and high spirits, they trooped back to thc kitchen. They would watch the ovens and kettles while the ladies had a turn at the sauna.

An hour later Mrs. Ek and Mrs. Rekkonen put the finishing touches to the feast and everyone stood at his place at the table, smiling in the lamplight.

"*Hauskaa Joulua*"—"Happy Yuletide"—they said to one another. Then for Mrs. Rekkonen, because this had been her family's custom in Sweden, they joined hands around the table while asking a blessing on the day and for the future.

The meal consisted of dishes made from traditional

Finnish recipes, many of which his own mother had cooked at various times, Toivo saw when finally the feast began. A huge bowl of boiled potatoes covered with cream sauce and sprinkled with allspice held the center position on the table. On a great blue platter lay thick pink slices of ham to be served with lingonberry relish. There were turnips both mashed and baked, fluffy boiled codfish, rice cooked with sugar and almonds, pastry tarts filled with apple and prune. And there was coffee with cookies and little frosted cakes. It was beautiful, gay, friendly. How Toivo wished he could join in the fun going on all around him! He tried.

"How about thtraw heaven, Papa?" little Selina asked her father two or three times; and the way in which he answered her, Toivo thought, gave importance to the question. Everything was arranged, Mr. Rekkonen assured his little girl, and she would have plenty of help so that "straw heaven" would be ready on time.

Wonder what that could be? Toivo thought, but soon forgot his question.

When the meal was over and the afternoon stretched ahead with several hours before the time when Father Christmas could be expected to arrive, it became clear, however, what Selina had meant.

The "heaven" was a straw mat or canopy. It was to be woven by hand and hung low beneath the ceiling of the parlor—or "*pirtti*," as Mrs. Ek said, using the old-country expression for this room.

Olli was shocked. "Not weaving! For boys?" His mother glanced around, her eyes full of mischief, pretending that she could not tell from what corner of the room his voice had come.

"Ay tought Ay heard someting. Someone vants no presents dis jear?"

"Aw." Olli knew that she was teasing, but that he was nonetheless caught. "I was plannin' to go coastin'."

"Da sleigh ride tomorrow," Mrs. Rekkonen whispered, rumpling his hair with affection, "vill be more fun, ya? For a boy who today makes his sister happy?"

"Hm," observed Olli. He sat cross-legged on the floor on which at that moment his father emptied a heap of straw and cord. The other children came to join him.

Darkness had fallen and candles were lit in the house before the weaving was finished, and even then silver stars were yet to be cut and pasted on the "heaven" before it was hung overhead. Candlelight reflected from the paper stars. The noisy talk and laughter quieted. Selina began to walk on tiptoe from window to window, trying to see out into the darkness. It was getting near time for Father Christmas.

"Real thoon he'll be here," Selina said, flattening her nose against the glass, her blue eyes growing rounder as time ticked by; and for once her voice was hushed. "Real thoon, I think."

There will be presents for her, Toivo said to himself, remembering other Christmas Eves, when he had been the waiting child. Tonight, Doctor Smith in boots and a red suit would bring gifts and a shower of candies; but for Toivo when he was little, Hadge had been the one. He felt that now the party was over for him.

I'll just slip out without disturbing the fun, he decided. I can say my thanks tomorrow.

In a flurry of excitement caused by the arrival of a

sleigh in the yard, he was able to leave unnoticed by a rear door, and in a few minutes had crossed the runway to the home float. Behind him he heard the swelling sound of voices as the front door of the Ek house opened to admit Father Christmas, then the muffling of sounds as the door closed again. Quickly he went into his own house.

Avoiding a glance at the window where Joe used to look in on him, Toivo undressed, crept into bed, and drew the blankets tight about his shoulders. Then, for all his need of sleep, he lay wide awake. In his mind was a stubborn vision, an expanse of ocean stretching beyond sight, and in this vastness one young sea lion.

When Aarni rang the bell outside half an hour later, he had only a moment to wait before Toivo opened the door.

"You comin' back, Toiv?" Aarni held his lantern high so that it shone on his friend, and he saw that he had been to bed. "Guess not."

"Thought I'd catch a little shuteye. Have to get up early in the morning so as not to miss the race."

"Sure. Well, Uncle Sam sent me to tell you there's no need to come to work in the morning, because there are plenty of us to get things done."

"Thanks, Aarn. See you in church, then."

"Right." Aarni's big boots took him back again to the Eks' door, where Toivo could hear the sound of stamping to clean them of snow, and hear the singing from inside the house, loud, then softened when the door opened and closed. His friend's lantern had reminded him that he should have set a lantern out for his father, since Hadge had not carried one with him; and quickly he lit the larger of the two at hand, adjusted the flame, set the light outside so that it shone on the snowy planking. Then, teeth chattering, he leaped back between his blankets; but scarcely had he turned over when the bell jangled again.

"Cousin Eb," it was this time—Doctor Smith, bringing the package that Toivo had not been there to receive from Father Christmas.

"Hi, in there, open up a shake!" the doctor had called. But when he saw the shivering boy who answered the call he thrust the package into his hands and spun away. "Get the dickens back into that bunk!"

"Thanks for this present, Doctor!"

"You skedaddle!"

Clutching the package that showed through its white paper wrapping its contents of red woolen mittens, Toivo made another leap for his covers. Then the bell rang again. He groaned and swung his feet from the bed.

Blazes! The doctor must have forgotten to say something or other. For the third time he paddled across the cold floor and opened the door; but at first he did not see anyone. Then—he was sure someone stood there in the shadows. It was Doctor Smith, wasn't it? Why didn't he say something?

Uneasily Toivo wished he could get hold of the lantern he had set out and could turn its light on his visitor.

"Who's there, anyway?" he called. Still the silence.

Then some small sound—something—told him!

Hardly believing, his heart pounding crazily, he whispered a name that he had thought he never again would say: "Joe?" Then wildly he shouted it, "JOE!" He leaped from the doorway, fell to his knees, his arms around the silent figure, and pressed his face against the whiskered face before him.

TEN

Halfway between laughter and tears, unmindful of the snow or of anything except this miracle of the young sea lion's return, Toivo failed at first to note that he was not getting the usual response from his pet.

"Joe, Joe," he kept saying, running his hands over the funny awkward body, roughing the frost-encrusted hair, "oh Joe, you're *home* again!" Finally the stiffness and lack of response were apparent to him. The little sea lion had not made any of his "talking" sounds or his glad swaying motions. This was mystifying. Toivo reached for the lantern. He held the light high and tried to peer into Joe's face. The big eyes turned away from him, looking off into the darkness.

"Now listen here!" The boy set the lantern down again. "I didn't want to go and leave you that day!" He caught his breath and loudly sneezed. "I hoped— maybe you'd know that." Again silence was his reply. He leaned and brushed the snow from his knees, began to shake violently with chill; then he reached out a hand to pet and stroke and asked an old question through his chattering teeth. "Joe," he asked, "want dinner, boy? Fish?"

"You're *talking!*" The big eyes swung around to him.

The faraway look brightened into eagerness; and suddenly Joe lunged forward. *"Ah-hoowr!"* he shouted, and came close to bowling Toivo overboard in his rush for the house! The door slammed shut behind the two of them. Toivo slipped into his shoes, pulling on his clothes.

"Hold everything!" He was laughing—excited and happy. "There're some fish in the boat. I'll get 'em!" Gone and back in a rush, he brought with him the fish and also a piece of canvas. "Food and a dry tarp!" he exulted; then hurriedly spread a meal for Joe, who snatched up the pieces of fish almost before they were out of Toivo's hands.

"Didn't you stop to eat, all that time?" The boy shook his head, watching. "What did you do—just start right out for home the minute they dumped you—and keep swimming? Joe?" Joe was too busy to answer him. Toivo spread the canvas across the foot of his bed.

For a long while that Christmas Eve (long after Joe himself was asleep on the canvas at Toivo's feet) the boy lay in bed listening to the young animal's peaceful breathing and waiting to hear Hadge's footsteps when he returned from the Eks' party. His first happiness at seeing Joe began to dim in the remembrance that his father was not likely to feel the same way that he did about this return. There was an end to Hadge Jarvenin's patience. The painful realization came to Toivo that now the problem of "what to do about Joe" must be faced all over again and that the problem had increased greatly; for, blazes, what was there left that could be done—to save him?

There isn't—anything, that I know of, the boy thought sadly. But there *has* to be something. Finally, before his father returned, he fell asleep; and it would have been difficult to waken him in the next few hours. When morning came and he did open his eyes, and saw that his father's bed was empty, then found that the *Gull* was gone, it seemed to him that at some time in the night he had been dimly aware of Hadge's presence beside his bed as the big man stared down at Joe, sleeping.

Had Hadge Jarvenin been glad as he stood there, and touched with wonder, as his son had been? Or was he filled with anger? Where had he gone before daybreak on a holiday morning—in a motorboat—without his breakfast?

Toivo looked at the clock. Five-thirty. Outside, it was still dark. Even with good lights it would be hard to keep the *Gull* clear of the trash coming down river. An hour from now, when the race was due to start, they still expected to use lanterns. Toivo was to be lantern boy for the Eks' sleigh. Aarni would carry the light for his own father's rig.

Well, the thing to do right now, Toivo decided, was to keep his mind on the fun ahead, instead of letting worry swamp him. For this one day, anyway, Joe was safe. And of course his father would return in time for the sleigh ride to church, the exciting finish to the old-country celebration, because he knew how much Toivo looked forward to it.

With resolution, then, the boy sat down in front of the stove, gazed through its isinglass window into the flames, and turned his thoughts where he wanted them to go:

to the moment when he would leap into the sleigh and start off, snow on his face and in his ears the sound of running horses' hoofs and the tinkle of harness bells.

He thought of what the kids had told him of the old-world custom of starting this day with a feast of lights. They would do that too, they said. Every window ledge of all the neighboring houses would hold a burning candle this morning. And since the schoolhouse was to be used for the church service, the windows there too would be candlelighted. Toivo had some difficulty in imagining that drab place touched by such magic.

Ten minutes before six. Still dark outside. He put coffee on the stove and sat down again.

The kids had said that for some reason the old-world villagers chose Christmas morning and the ride to church as the time to show off their finest, fastest horses. Aarni thought that this might be because everyone felt free from work and unusually gay; but Olli said, huh, they just wanted to be sure of getting home in a hurry to a holiday breakfast. Anyway, Toivo knew that his friends too had groomed their steeds until they shone and had polished harness and harness bells. For this event, American Finns too would speed magnificently over the countryside with their lanterns bobbing, bells ringing, bright-colored caps and scarves flying or held against the wind.

Six o'clock. Toivo began to pace from window to window. He'd had his own breakfast; his father's food waited for him. Joe, out on the deck, was sniffing at all things, busily re-establishing his ownership of the place.

"What do I do with you while I'm gone?" Toivo asked

the seal from the doorway. "Anything special?" Joe's reply was unconcerned.

"*Aw-hoowr,*" he tossed back lightly, "no problem." And he was right, for once. There would be no hunters out today—not before daylight on Christmas morning. Besides, this youngster was terribly tired, and he'd take a nap. Toivo felt sure of it.

Six-fifteen. Joe had gone to sleep, all right, inside near the door. If only he would stay there, now, and not get in Hadge's way. Toivo had filled the lantern he was to carry on the sleigh and had polished its glass chimney. Now he put on his jacket and cap and the new red gloves. They would still be able to make it—if his father came right away. He listened for the motorboat, watched the hands of the clock, until at six-twenty-five he heard the Rekkonen boys' voices as they talked to the horses and saw activity in the Eks' yard. A terrible cold weight seemed to come into his stomach, a premonition of trouble.

The two teams, he saw—Mr. Rekkonen's grays and Mr. Ek's brown Dick and Bonnie—had been brought with their sleighs to the kitchen porch of the farmhouse where the "Rauhallista" placard hung; and there the four horses pawed the snow and blew happy jets of vapor from their nostrils. Both families, except for the boys, waited in their sleighs. Olli and Aarni now, with, "What the dickens is the matter with the Jarvenins!" written on their faces, were sprinting toward the houseboat. There was no sound of the *Gull.*

"Too late." Toivo stood very still, accepted this reality. Then he took off his jacket, cap, and gloves and opened the door as Aarni and Olli skidded to a stop in front of Joe. Openmouthed, the brothers stared at the sea lion; and politely Joe arose to say "how-do" to them.

"He—swam—back," marveled Aarni. "Just—swam—right—back—again." One of his hands unbelievingly touched Joe's head. Both brothers shook their round heads and looked for a long time at the adventurous sea lion. At last they turned their eyes from him to Toivo, and in one word condensed all their feeling. "Gosh." Olli recalled their reason for being there.

"Then you aren't goin' to ride the race?" he asked; and Toivo shook his head. It would be all right, he thought, to let the boys think that Joe was his reason for staying home. He couldn't explain his father's absence to them, since he himself didn't understand that. He thrust his lantern into Olli's hands.

"Carry this for the Eks, will you, Ol?" The younger boy nodded, seemingly dazed, but he took hold of the lantern handle. He and Aarni walked away. When they had gone part of the distance back across the planking, they suddenly sprang into action, raced the rest of the way to the waiting sleighs, and jumped to their places.

It was six-thirty on the dot. The sleighs started off. For a while Toivo's eyes could follow them over the snow, then the mist came between. Soon even the tinkle of the harness bells was gone.

Hadge came in quietly; but he was not in a quiet mood. When he saw Toivo he scowled and hid something behind him.

"What are you doing here?" he demanded. "I thought you were to go with the Eks."

"While you were out on the river?" Toivo had been

watching for the meeting between his father and Joe; but there had been no such meeting. Instead, Joe had drawn away, and Hadge had come past him without a glance in his direction. Then the big man had slipped whatever he was carrying to a hiding place behind the gramophone and hurriedly drunk the coffee that Toivo had made for him.

"You should have gone!" Hadge fumed. "I had no wish for you to miss what you were interested in." His hair stuck every which way from under the Laplander cap.

"Both of us," Toivo pointed out, "missed the sleigh ride." He called up a little more courage. "Father," he asked, "why did you walk past Joe just now as if you didn't see him?"

"Don't think I *didn't see him!*"

"And he dodged back"—Toivo was puzzled—"afraid of you!" Hadge's dark scowl deepened.

"Animals sense—"

"Sense what? I don't seem to—"

"Sense—what must be."

Alarm shot through Toivo. He leaned forward, searched Hadges's face. "Why," he asked sharply, "did you want me to be gone when you came back? Why did you—" He crossed the room, looked behind the gramophone. There lay a revolver! His father had gone this morning to borrow this, and bring it home with him.

"What's going on!" His cry was stricken. He knew.

"We must end this, boy. Once and for all, we must have it over with. Both of us did all we could—arranged to take the animal back where he came from, but he will not stay there. There is no other way."

123

"Let him stay with me—just for a while! I'll think of something else—beside this! I will! I promise!"

"Now I'm not going to have you making things tougher than they are. You go over to the Eks. Stay there a while. I'll call you, later."

"Father! No!"

"I am a good shot. Your seal will not know."

"You are wrong! I know you are—"

"Don't question me! No Finn boy—"

"I'm not a Finn boy! How many times do I have to tell you that? You are the Finn—you and your cap—" Toivo heard his own voice shouting, was shocked by its wildness, but could not stop the flow of words. "You—"

"Quiet!" Hadge's eyes were flashing. Roughly he propelled the now struggling Toivo through the door and turned him in the direction of the runway. Somehow in the struggle the Laplander cap fell from Hadge's head into the snow.

"That cap!" Toivo wanted to hurt him. "The way you talk! I'm not going to be like that! Go on back to your country, and I'll stay here. I'll take care of myself and Joe too!"

They had come to the edge of the float where the runway started; but Toivo would not go across it. He set his feet as brakes.

"On your way!" Hadge too was shouting.

"I won't do it!"

The big man's arm swung back, delivered a blow to the side of Toivo's face that staggered him and sent him reeling against the post where the bell hung; and by this post he righted himself. He shook his head to clear it.

The swing of that blow, he saw now, must also have

staggered his father. Or had Hadge tripped on the pile of nets?

His father was falling! He struck his head on the edge of the float and rolled into the water!

ELEVEN

"He can't swim! God help him, he can't swim!" Toivo threw himself down at the float's edge and strained to see through the shroud of mist lying over the river; but at first he was unable to make out even the surface of the water. Was his father in sight? Trying to help himself? There was no way of knowing!

His second thought was more comforting: I can get him out, all right—easily reach him! He braced himself, tensing to give the wet and angry man a hand up to the float; but time went by, a terribly long time, and no sound came from Hadge, neither a call nor a splashing about. He had not come to the surface!

The boy saw at the moment two things to send horror chilling through him and to let him wait no longer. He glimpsed a filigree of blood upon the water and saw a piece of fish net momentarily floating, then pulled down as though by weight. Where these were, Toivo dived deep.

Dark. The water was deadly cold—and dark. To open one's eyes was painful, almost useless. It would be easy to be trapped down here. Had his father been caught in this sticky mud? Tangled in that piece of net?

He felt his way, groping hands touching nothing, tortured eyes glimpsing only snags and trash in the river: cans, rusty cables about pilings. Forced to come up for air, he was almost instantly down again.

Don't panic—easy does it, he kept saying to himself. You've got to force your eyes to open. Then he touched a cloth jacket—glimpsed a white face in the water—had hold of his father!

Hadge's body had been lying deep, the net entangling him. Toivo took a rescue hold, one arm about the drowning man's head, and trod as best he could toward the surface of the river; but the going was slow. He was so dog tired. That suction in under the float—hard to resist. The boy knew that he was not doing well.

He wasn't doing well at all! His lungs were going to burst. He had reached the limit of his endurance!

Don't panic, he tried to tell himself; but choked and took in water. A roaring came in his head. He himself seemed to be part of the river and one with it—carried along—whirling, whirling . . . They were to die, then, he and his father? This—was—the—end? He almost let go his grasp on Hadge. It loosened, but something —some feeling that Old River himself might be helping —made Toivo renew his hold. Suddenly, strangely, his own weight and his father's weight seemed less. Suddenly both of them were moving upward, rushed and pushed upward through tortuous green depths—and had broken the surface of the water!

Toivo could breathe! Could snatch the good—wonderful air in great gulps of thankfulness, tighten one arm about his unconscious burden, and with his other hand hold to the edge of the float!

He became aware after a while that the force which

had so miraculously lifted him from death was still close by—under him, about him, a tan shape of incredible skill in water and eyes of unfailing devotion. Joe, of course. Up to his old tricks!

"C-crazy galoot!" Thankfulness filled Toivo's whisper. New courage flowed through him. Calling upon his remaining strength, he held to the float, kept his father's head above water.

Someone would come. He knew someone would come now and help. Now, he wasn't going to give up.

Aarni always claimed afterward that he'd had a "hunch" that something was wrong at the Jarvenin house when he and Olli and Toivo were talking at the door before the sleigh ride started and had learned that Joe was back; and he said that it was because of this hunch that he'd gone hustling over there again when the sleighs returned to the Eks' dooryard.

However it was, and for whatever reason, Aarni's coming set in motion forces that brought needed help to Toivo and Hadge.

Everybody at the farmhouse came running when Aarni shouted. They pulled Hadge and Toivo from the river, while Joe flipped into an extra, self-congratulatory dive, then scrambled out to join in the excitement. Toivo, they rushed into the house for hot drinks and hot blankets; but with Hadge they dared not waste a moment. Doctor Smith began working with him as he lay right there on the float, trying to make his lungs function. It took a long, long time, but at last Hadge drew his own breath. At last he could be put in bed, piled with blankets, surrounded with jars of hot water.

"But he doesn't seem to know what is going on." Toivo came to lean over his father. "His head is hurt too."

"I'm going to take care of the wound, all right," promised Doctor Smith. "It looks as though it may have been made by a nail as he fell. But it is not that injury I am concerned about. It's the shock he is in. I'll stay close by tonight."

The day passed, then the night; but Hadge neither spoke nor moved, only lay on his back as they had placed him, his eyes closed. Except for the time it took to fetch wood and water and to feed Joe, Toivo did not leave his father's bedside.

"What do you do for patients like this?" the boy asked painfully. "What helps?"

"For some reason, your father is making no effort to return to us. And, frankly, we need that effort from him." The doctor turned and gazed out the window, frowning, thoughtful. "You said he tripped? And that's what caused his fall?"

"I think he must have."

"Wasn't running, overly excited, anything like that?"

"Father was—walking," Toivo replied carefully, frowning too, remembering how Hadge had been.

"I suppose—" The doctor sighed and turned back from the window. "He has perhaps had enough, with the blood poisoning and being unable to work for so long and all, to make him like this—"

"Perhaps." Toivo nodded, but added in his own thoughts, Only you don't really think so, do you, Doctor? And I don't either. Once more he studied the face on the pillow. No ordinary concern such as those about ill health or money would have been enough to quiet this once-defiant spirit, he knew. It would have taken a hurt to the heart, such as the one his son had dealt him, to quiet Hadge Jarvenin.

"I am to blame." Toivo faced his own accusation. "I said things—that never should have been said—childish things. And I put Joe first, and my father last." He leaned close.

Was he too late? Too late in growing up?

"Papa," he murmured, the small-boy term slipping from him without his knowing, "I was wrong. Hear me —please. I know you were not thinking of yourself, but of me. I'll go with you—anywhere you think best." There was no response. It seemed that Hadge was hardly breathing. Brokenheartedly Toivo touched the reindeer-hide cap that someone had picked up from the snow and laid on the bed, put his cheek against it. He did not see Hadge's eyes open, but after a moment heard the murmur of his voice.

"Someday," the voice was saying, "maybe you'll wear that a little—just now and then." Toivo's head jerked erect! His father was looking at him. And in that dark gaze a spark of laughter flickered. From somewhere Hadge Jarvenin had come back!

"Wear—your cap, Father?"

"That—is bad?"

"That is *good!*" Toivo laughed aloud, clasped his father's hand. "I'll wear it any time! HYVAA! [Good!]"

"I . . . no more," murmured Hadge, and turned as though he would have said something further, but sighed and dropped into restful sleep, leaving his words unspoken. Doctor Smith, examining him, straightened up, well satisfied.

"Fine." He nodded. "He will be all right." Then he motioned to Toivo that he would like to speak with him outside.

"What do you think he meant by that 'no more' of his?" asked the doctor. "No more what?"

"It had me scared," Toivo admitted, "for a minute."

"We need some things from the drugstore. Can you take the *Gull* to Astoria and get them?"

"Sure!"

"They'll amount to a couple of dollars. I can let you have—"

"Thanks." Toivo's mind went at once to the sugar bowl. "I have it, all right."

"Hop along then." The doctor took off his glasses, put them on again, then wrote a list of supplies and gave it to Toivo with a small, heavy package that he said belonged to the man who worked for the druggist and should be returned to him.

The good man sent a glance riverward, once more took off his glasses and put them on again. "You—will be a sharp navigator, hm?" He meant, "Take care."

Toivo felt relieved to get away from home anxieties for a while. He had taken the money from the bowl, put the doctor's list safely in his shirt pocket, and laid on the seat of the boat the package he was to deliver. Then he'd whistled for Joe, since he had no choice but to take the seal with him. This would work out all right, though. The drugstore where he intended to go was close to the landing slip in town, and there would be only a short distance to walk. Besides, he would be glad to have good company on the long boat run. Joe had lolloped aboard as though he'd expected the invitation all along.

They made the trip to Astoria without incident and the young seal, at least, had a pleasant time of it. Here he was, Joe's cheerful manner seemed to say, right out here in the wind and tide and mist that he liked, with his best friend for a companion. What more could a sea lion ask? Toivo, on the other hand, had felt the wind biting through his thin jacket, and suffered with feet like ice in his wet shoes. He was relieved to sight Fisher's slip.

After he had made the *Gull* fast and he and Joe had walked up the slippery incline to the street, the shivering boy would have delighted in a cup of hot coffee. He told himself, though, that on a cold day like this those eating places were sure to be crowded. They were no place for Joe. He warmed himself instead by jumping up and down and flailing his arms.

People on the street turned to look and some of them to smile at the sight of the boy and his pet seal. One young man who carried a camera slung over his shoulder seemed more than casually interested, and strolled along beside Toivo, asking questions. He was a pleasant young fellow. At first Toivo enjoyed telling him about Joe's many tricks and of the way he acted when people were in swimming. He was relating the account of Joe's return home after being put out at sea, and of his rescue of Hadge and himself, when the uncomfortable certainty came over him that he wasn't being believed. He turned away from his new companion.

"I talk too much!" he said. But the young man would not let him walk away.

"Do you suppose," he asked, "if I could get up your way today, that either your Mr. Ek or Doctor Smith would talk with me?"

"Talk with you? Why not? What is your name?"

"Sorry. My bad manners. The name is Cameron. Jeff. I work for a news syndicate but have been down this way on vacation. Have to catch the afternoon train for Portland."

"I'm Toivo Jarvenin." They shook hands, and Toivo felt more kindly toward Mr. Cameron. "I don't know why people wouldn't want to talk with you."

The young man chuckled. "There are those who don't." He made you feel like smiling with him, the boy thought, but for all that, his eyes were sharp. Now he was showing a leather card case on the cover of which were printed his own name and that of his news syndicate.

"You are welcome to ride with Joe and me in the boat," said Toivo.

"Good deal. Where do I meet you?"

"Foot of the slip back there." Toivo gestured with his thumb. "In a few minutes." With Joe at his heels he turned in then at the drugstore, noticing that the man behind the counter squinted a critical eye at his sea-lion customer and the wet track behind him on the floor, but Joe squinted right back at him and kept coming until he reached the counter and could press close to Toivo's legs.

"I'd like these things, please." Toivo handed the doctor's list to the man, and while he read it secretly rubbed Joe's stomach with his foot to congratulate him. Then he laid the small, heavy package on the counter. It had the owner's name written on it. "Is this person here?"

"I'll call him for you."

Apparently wondering what this was about, the other clerk came and began to unwrap the package that the doctor had sent; but when he saw what it contained thrust it, paper and all, into his coat pocket. He had seen Joe outside the counter, and now he leaned forward for a longer look at him and a puzzled glance at Toivo.

"Yeah," he avowed at last, shrugged, and turned away.

Toivo too had seen the package's contents as the man opened it, and he knew now why the doctor had thought it best to get the object out of the house. He must also have wondered why it was there. The package held the revolver that Hadge had borrowed to shoot Joe.

"That clerk will never be able to figure it out, Joe." Toivo touched the young sea lion's round head as they came out onto the street. "He had the look on his face that the stories always call 'baffled.'"

In a short while they were on their way upriver, Toivo and Joe and Mr. Cameron. Wrapped in his overcoat, the young man sat in the boat's stern, alternately smoking his pipe and dozing. Joe, quite as peaceful, snoozed nearby.

The *Gull* ran well. There was not too much trouble with river drift. Now and then Toivo took off one of his gloves, rubbed his arms and hands as well as he could without letting go of the tiller; and a little resentment grew in him at the way the tables were being turned.

He had thought on this trip home to become the questioner instead of the questioned, to find out more about this city man and the life he lived and why he was here; but Jeff Cameron was giving few answers.

Once when the boat passed near a certain spot, in hope that his passenger would tell a tale of his own adventures, Toivo remarked that this was the place where he had first found young Joe. At another time when he thought of the way the lights looked out in the channel during fishing season he'd asked if Mr. Cameron had seen the night life in any big cities. Both efforts at conversation had turned somehow into one-sided affairs with Toivo doing the talking. Finally Mr. Cameron was left to doze and smoke in peace. Questions, however, did not stop buzzing in the boy's head.

What the dickens, he wondered does a big man like this want from Mr. Ek or the doctor? What could be so important that he's willing to trek up here for it in the middle of winter?

His curiosity was in no way lessened when he realized that his young man was not actually as sleepy as he pretended to be. Every now and again Toivo caught the gleam of half-shut eyes watching him.

TWELVE

"That's the place, there." Toivo spoke shortly to the newsman who had been his passenger. They stepped out onto the float and Joe flopped from his nap in the boat to a place beside them. Toivo began to tie up and indicated the Ek house with a nod over one shoulder.

"Mm-hm." Young Cameron's eyes were cool. He shoved his hands deep into his pockets and started off, talking as he went. "I'll go on over, then. They have a phone, don't they?"

"Yes, they do."

"Thanks for the ride, skipper."

"Okay, Mr. Cameron." Toivo went into the house, closing the door behind Joe, who rocked in after him, sure of welcome, and set down the package of medicines. His father was sleeping. At the moment no one else was there.

He took off his jacket, laid cap and mittens beside it and sat down by the stove to warm his feet and wait for Hadge to waken. Joe, sensing the mood of silence, waited too, and watched soundlessly from a position at the foot of the bed.

As he waited the boy's mind wandered. He noticed the firm bandage that Doctor Smith had put over his father's head wound and noticed too that the sick man had been given a shave; and that his wild hair had been so closely trimmed that he no longer gave the appearance of having too large a head. How much younger he looked!

Doctors know how to do a lot of different things, I guess, thought Toivo. Country doctors, anyway. He followed his thoughts on through the events of Christmas morning: Joe dodging away from Hadge when he came back from his trip to borrow the revolver, his own wild rebellion, Hadge's fall, Joe's wonderful rescue of the two of them. Did his father realize, Toivo wondered, that his life and his son's had been saved by the animal he had been going to destroy?

His thoughts came to the words his father had muttered when first he regained consciousness: "Maybe you'll wear [the cap] a little?" and "I—no more."

"He was trying to tell me something important. Something he decided not to do—or say. Could it have been about the old cap? That he is not going to wear that any more as a symbol of his failure to Americanize? Did he try to say he would no more return to the scow? No more plan to go back to the old country? Or—was it something about Joe? Whatever he had—or has—in mind, how will it now change our lives?

Once more Toivo's eyes rested on his father's face. It seemed to him for the moment peaceful, and the boy's restless thoughts quieted. Then, since he was tired, he too slipped into a doze.

After a while the ringing of the bell outside and footsteps at the door brought an end to this quiet time.

Toivo jumped awake and Hadge opened his eyes as Doctor Smith entered, followed by the young newspaperman who had come upriver with Toivo. The doctor's face was beaming with more than bedside cheerfulness. What was he so tickled about? Toivo wondered.

"Wouldn't have interrupted your sleep, Hadge," Doctor Smith declared, "except that it is medicine time, anyway, and you've an important visitor." He introduced the two men, and Toivo exchanged nods with his former passenger, noting again the keenness behind the twinkle in his eyes.

"Plenty of time for sleeping," Hadge told him good-naturedly. He put his arms under his head to prop it up. "Good afternoon," he said to Jeff Cameron. When Toivo pushed chairs forward and his father saw him for the first time since his return from Astoria the big man looked relieved. "Back safely, eh?"

"Yes." Toivo gave his father a long, long look and knew that he sounded as startled as he was feeling; for the sentences his father just now had spoken were different from his usual speech. They had come from him in almost smooth English and with less accent than could be attained by most English-speaking Finns. Was it possible, Toivo asked himself, that this stubborn man could have improved his speech any time he wished? Could this change have been part of what he had meant by his mysterious words, "I—no more"? Why then was he choosing this particular time of low ebb in their fortunes, when he himself threatened to leave America as a poor risk, to become more—not less—Americanized?

"Yes, I'm home," he said again. "The *Gull* behaved well." He saw that young Cameron's gaze, which had been roaming the room, now came to rest upon Joe, still quiet at the foot of the bed and partly hidden by over-hanging covers, but quivering from snout to tail with hope for attention.

Blazes, now he'll start talking about Joe! Toivo told himself that if he'd had a lick of sense he would not have brought the seal into the house. He had grave doubts about his father's reaction to the creature who had brought him so much trouble. (Trouble, but what a lot of luck—if only he knew it!) Sure enough, the newsman began.

"All members of your family," he said brightly, "seem to be present and accounted for, Mr. Jarvenin." Toivo held his breath. He saw his father's gaze go slowly to Joe while the sea lion looked steadfastly back at him, saw their glances lock. The boy could have kicked himself!

This didn't have to happen! You didn't have to let Joe get right under his nose! he stormed in his thoughts at his own carelessness. As if things weren't bad enough already! He started to motion to Joe, to take him out-side, but a motion of his father's hand stopped him. A faint humorous twitching had begun at the corners of Hadge's mouth while he exchanged stares with Joe; and now, for the newsman's information, he began to explain the sea lion.

"*This* member of my family," announced Hadge Jar-venin in his slow, deep voice with little hesitancy for words, as a half smile flickered on his face and he ges-tured grandly, "is my cousin, Joe Whiskers. Joe—well, he is the relative we can neither live with—nor without."

He knows! exulted Toivo. He knows, all right, that Joe saved us.

"*Aw-hoowr,*" objected the young sea lion, ducking his head with such plainly false modesty that everyone had to laugh; and Jeff Cameron must jump to his feet and begin to unstrap his camera.

"It is all right to take pictures, isn't it?" He looked from the doctor to Hadge.

"Medically, yes." The doctor nodded. "If the head of the house agrees, you can come back in about five minutes, Mr. Cameron."

"Of course." Young Cameron took a step toward the door, and came to a stop, looking at Hadge's collection of carved wooden figures on the shelf behind the stove. He gave a long, low whistle. "This," he declared, "is probably the most unusual family I shall ever know." He tossed a grin over his shoulder at Hadge, gesturing in the direction of the figurines. "More of your relatives, Mr. Jarvenin?" He waved and moved on out. "See you later."

The doctor had wanted to talk with Hadge and to give him his medicine. Toivo grasped the opportunity for asking the questions churning around inside him.

"This Mr. Cameron," he said to Doctor Smith, "is he your friend or Mr. Ek's? Why does he want to take pictures? Why does he think we are so unusual? What did he come way up here for?"

"Do you think, Toiv"—the doctor was slowly, carefully pouring medicine from bottle to spoon—"that you might back up and start over again?" He gave the medicine to his patient, then answered one question. "It seems to me," he said, "that the young man is *your* friend, if he is anyone's."

"Mine!"

"No," said Hadge, making a face at the medicine's taste. "He is not even a Finn."

"All friends are not Finns, my friend. This Cameron is an American newspaperman."

"From the land of opportunity," Hadge mocked, slipping momentarily into his old bitterness, sparking a quick response from Eb Smith.

"Right you are!" Then he laughed. "Well, Cousin Elin has invited Mr. Cameron to dinner. You know what that means!"

"Means she's pretty darn sure he's worth the trouble!" Toivo answered for his father. Now he saw again on the big man's face that flick of a smile. Some of the doctor's good humor and that feeling of excitement behind everything he said this morning was affecting them all, the boy thought. Hadge, however, had more to ask about Jeff Cameron.

"The man writes for newspapers, you say?" The way he voiced the question put newswriters in a class with swindlers.

"He writes, yes." The doctor was enjoying himself. "For a syndicate of papers, as it happens. From the credentials he showed us over at the house I would say you could trust him."

Toivo, putting wood in the stove, added his comment. "I liked him. Though part of the time he did seem to be sort of spying on me. Funny, he started off by telling me he was down this way on vacation, but ended by ask-

141

ing for a ride here to talk with you or Mr. Ek. Didn't say what about."

"About you, of course. And about Joe."

"What in blazes for?"

"For a good human-interest yarn to take back with him—provided it turned out to be true." The doctor chuckled. "When you began to tell him about Joe's long trek home again from outside the bar, and followed up with an account of his rescue of the two of you from the river, he thought he had better— Well—" The doctor shrugged.

"Thought I was telling whoppers, hm?"

"Let's say he wasn't sure."

Toivo laughed. "Now what?"

"Oh, now he's building up a head of steam. He is all on your side; and I suspect he is set to write the prize-winning story of the year about your seal."

"You're fooling."

"A little." The doctor once more turned his attention to Hadge. "I do believe this, though: that if you two people will give him permission to write his article without restrictions, you are in for a dilly of a surprise."

"Tokko! [I wonder!]" The Finnish exclamation seemed to have burst from Hadge.

"Something bothers you?"

"You said, 'without restrictions.' Do you want this peddler to—to—" Hadge almost choked on his indignation but became calmer. "This writer of yours would put us in his paper, humorous characters, to make for himself the money, Doctor. Our 'strange old customs'—'the peculiar people' to be found here in our settlement. You

142

must know this! Do you think there is money enough to pay us for such a thing?"

"Hey!" Toivo's voice now held alarm. "Thinking of that—I don't like it either."

"Well, it isn't that way." Doctor Smith took off his glasses, put them on again. "My stars, it isn't that way at all."

"Father is right." Toivo spoke with finality.

The doctor chuckled and threw his crossed arms in front of his face as though to ward off a blow.

"Will both of you listen a minute? I *know* we don't want tags as a peculiar people. I belong here too, in case anyone cares to remember it." Then he spoke seriously. "I'm sure you know that I am your friend—and admirer. I want to see you have your chance, and this may be it. Come on, let me call young Cameron in here, let him explain what he has in mind."

"Wish you would!" That was the returning newsman's voice. "First, though—" He walked to the shelf of carvings and took one of them in his hand. It was the one Toivo liked best, because it reminded him of the red-haired young man on the scow that morning who had declared himself on the side of sea lions. "I could sell these for you, Mr. Jarvenin."

Hadge looked unbelieving. "Someone would buy those?"

"No doubt about it." Jeff Cameron set the figure back in its place. "You would have to trust me with them, of course, and they would not bring so much at first as they will later on. But yes, sir! Someone will buy them, all right."

143

"While they stand there," said Hadge, "they bring nothing at all."

"You wish me to try?"

"I would thank you."

Not so fast, Mr. Newsman! Toivo did not say those words aloud. They were in his thoughts. He had stepped a little closer to his father, frowning. *This* Jarvenin is listening too!

Young Cameron was still talking. "You know"—he seated himself facing Hadge and his son and looked at them earnestly—"I wish you could trust me—believe me. It would give us so much more time. It's this way: a man like me meets many people. Comes to know certain things about them, the way they react to situations and so on, tells him usually if they are genuine or—humbugs. He learns another thing—that an ordinary workday with bare facts can also produce 'mysteries'—if you want to call them that. I mean, he sees that there are in the world certain unsolved and unexplained combinations of circumstances, and—" Jeff Cameron's laugh was somewhat self-conscious. He ran his hands over his head. "Wow. My skill with words seems to be taking a vacation."

"We follow pretty well," Toivo told him.

"Skipper." The young man turned to him. "Look at this from my point of view. Suppose for a minute that you are a man like me. You meet an old-world craftsman who has come to America to find a future for his family and for himself. In the same place you discover a boy, an American doctor-in-the-making, asking no favors but only a fair shake—and in still the same location you meet an intelligent and likable personality in the body

144

of a sea animal, who has arrived from the sea in the
nick of time to save the first two characters from death,
so that they may have futures. Well, don't you feel as I
do, that perhaps your hand too is meant to be included
in the drama? That you want very much to be the in-
strument to present this cast of distinguished players?"

Look out, Toivo warned himself. You are beginning to
like this man better and better.

"It may be hard for you to understand," the newsman
finished, "but I believe that a writer has a responsibility to take on such an assignment. And I believe that his
pride in a job like that would be evident in every word
he wrote." He took out his handkerchief and wiped his
face, then leaned back in his chair and waited. Toivo
watched his father. Hadge frowned at the floor, and for
a long moment said nothing; then he turned to Toivo.

"Do you consider," he asked his son, "that Cousin Joe
here is good story material?"

"The best!" Toivo heard himself answering. "He'd
make a humdinger!"

Newswriter Cameron went to work. With the smooth-
ness of an old hand he organized his day so that few
minutes would be lost. He had telephoned the hotel in
Astoria, he said, to put his luggage on the afternoon
train, and he himself would board that train when it
came through Svenson; but they would have time to re-
cord their story. If everyone would tell him things, show
him places, pose willingly for pictures, they'd make it in
time, all right.

"Only," said Toivo, feeling again the uncertainty that

hung over Joe, "the story won't have an ending. The story will stop right in the middle."

Young Cameron caught his meaning. "Because things are not settled yet for your sea lion?"

"They aren't, you know. Nothing is decided. There is no—answer."

"Fellow never can tell, Skipper. Sometimes there are —surprises." He and the doctor exchanged smiles and nods, and Toivo realized that they had a secret between them; but he felt that the secret could not include Joe. "I'll tell you right now," the writer continued, "that this whiskered pinniped named Joe Whiskers is going to keep his spot as my lead character."

"A story's different from the real thing."

"Let's give it time." Doctor Smith rumpled Toivo's shock of hair as he passed on his way into the house to pack. "'A little time and a little faith,' as Cousin Elin says." The doctor must go back now to his office and Aarni to his job on the boat. The holiday was over. They had arranged that Aarni would come by in the skiff so that they could go aboard the *Sue Elmore* together.

"As to that ending," Jeff Cameron said to Toivo, "no story ever does actually end, anyway. Ever think of that? All stories go on—leading into new developments, forever."

"In a way. But not for Joe."

Looking back afterward on that day, Toivo marveled at the speed with which it had flown. Hardly had he and Joe said good-by to the doctor and Aarni as those two skimmed down river in Aarni's skiff when they must splash through mud to wave young Cameron on his way

146

on the train with a box of six of the carvings under one arm and his camera slung over his shoulder. All of them had talked a great deal in the hours the newsman was with them. He had, as Mrs. Ek said, "Such a nice way about him."

In that backward glance afterward Toivo realized too that neither he nor his father nor any of the rest of them, except perhaps the doctor, had had any idea of the enormity of the change that was to come to them as a result of the talk.

Little more than a week after Jeff Cameron's train steamed up the tracks toward Portland, the first glimpse of what his visit was to mean for them began with a call on the Eks' kitchen telephone. Mrs. Ek answered it, then ran, panting, to the barn, where morning chores were under way.

"Long-distance call!" she managed to say. "Toivo! For you."

THIRTEEN

"This is Toivo Jarvenin!" Toivo loudly announced into the mouthpiece of the telephone. "Who is calling?"

"OUCH!"

"What?"

"*Ouch.*" The voice coming over the wire crackled amid static sounds, and the flustered boy looked quickly at both ends of the receiver to be sure that nothing there was wrong. He couldn't have heard what he thought he'd heard! No one said "ouch" over long distance. He pounded a few times on the wall box.

"Couldn't hear you very well!" he shouted above the sounds on the wire. "What did you say?" Suddenly the wire was quiet.

"Jeff Cameron speaking," stated a calm voice in this lull. "What's all the shouting?"

"Oh. Hello, Mr. Cameron." Toivo felt his face burn. He never before had used a telephone; but other people always seemed to shout into them. He guessed that Mr. Cameron was laughing at him.

"Seen any papers today, Skipper?"

"No, I haven't."

"Well, you get them!"

"Joe's story? Wow! Already?"

"Right. All about Joe Whiskers. Who else?"

"Which papers?"

"Whichever ones you can get hold of. More will be mailed to you. Now hear this. There's news for your father."

"Is it—good news?"

"It is. All six of those carvings I brought up here with me were sold before I'd gone outside the hotel lobby. Seven-fifty each. The money order is in this morning's mail."

"That's"—Toivo gulped—"*great!*"

"You ask him to mail some more carvings to me here right away, will you? I want to take them with me to Seattle."

"I'll— Sure I'll tell him."

"And tell him they will bring a better price after he is known."

"Think so?"

"Know so. You will box them up, hm? Get them up here?"

"Bet I will!"

"That's it, then, Skipper."

"Wait, Mr. Cameron!"

"Yes?"

"Thank you. From—the three of us."

"My pleasure."

Slowly, as though in a dream, Toivo hung up the receiver and turned to face Sam and Elin Ek standing there in the kitchen, without seeing them at all.

"Couldn't help hearin', Elin and me. Sounded pretty all-fired interesting!"

"Yes." Toivo rubbed his face, trying to come awake.

"*You know what that was about?*" he finally shouted, excitement mounting in him. "You know what's *happened?*"

"Newspaper fella's got Joe in the papers, hm?"

"And he's sold some of Father's carvings! Without trying, even. The money is in the mail!"

"Oh, that is going to mean a lot to your pa. An awful lot, boy."

"We are real happy about it," Mrs. Ek said; and she looked happy.

"I've got to get moving!" Now the excited boy was wide awake. He rushed to the door, remembered his cap lying on top of the phone box and rushed back again for that, then dashed out. "I'll finish the chores—on the double!"

"No, you won't!" Mr. Ek sounded as if he meant it. The running feet stopped.

"No more chores today. You be on your way, boy."

"But you—"

"On your way!" Mr. Ek shooed him down the steps; and his laughter as he leaped to the ground and began to run was thanks enough for the little man. To Joe the sea lion, who had been waiting outside for his boy to come, the change of routine was an annoyance that brought a scolding rumble from him. He leaped after the running feet, slapped through the slush, rocked across the runway; but before he could catch the speeding Toivo the house door slammed in his face. For once, Toivo had forgotten him.

Hadge had gone to sleep with his face to the wall that morning after an early breakfast lacking substance in some respects. Toivo had kept thinking as he prepared the light meal that luckily this was payday for him at the Eks' and that the money would buy a few of the things he and his father needed. He could get salt and pancake flour and matches, and he hoped some coal oil. Now, as he ran into the room with the wonderful news of the sale of the carvings, he knew that they would be able to afford far more than this. Why, they would be able to buy all the food they would need for a long while.

"You just had a call on the telephone, Father! About your carvings!" He saw the sleeping man stir and turn his head part way to listen.

"Your carvings. They sold! Jeff Cameron sold all six of them and he didn't even go outside the hotel to do it. The money is in the mail right now!" He paused for breath and to hear what Hadge would say; but the man on the bed said nothing.

Toivo leaned over him. "What's the matter? Don't you—" He did not finish his question, and in a moment tiptoed away. A man had a right to shed tears—even happy tears of relief—in private.

On the float deck, Joe had to wait some time for attention, though he pressed his most reproachful face against the glass of the front window and stared inside. Toivo's thoughts seemed to be far away from those about him. The seal watched the boy make coffee, saw that he and his father drank a good deal of it and talked in an excited way, laughing aloud every now and then, and saw Toivo take some of the wooden figurines from behind the stove and put them in a packing box. At last, carrying the box, Toivo came out the door; and Joe rocketed to meet him, ready for anything.

"You wouldn't stay here, I suppose, Joe, while I walk up the tracks to the store," Toivo said. "Would you, boy?"

"*Aw-hoowr,*" replied Joe.

"I didn't think so." The way the seal's eyes twinkled and he romped to the runway and back had been answer enough without his "word." The boy lifted his feet one at a time and examined his shoes. The soles of both of them had holes, of course. "Oh, well, my feet are soaked anyway, little more isn't going to make much difference. We'll take the path."

"*Ah-woor!* [Righto!]" agreed Joe, and led the way.

Snow still lay on the path to the store, which for most of the way ran parallel to the tracks but now and then ran in under trees and tree branches heavy with the white stuff. Joe welcomed every cascade of snow with cavortings of joy, but Toivo turned up his jacket collar and stepped aside to avoid them.

"You'd make a picture for Mr. Cameron now," he told the snow covered Joe, with white beads on those long eyelashes—white cape on your shoulders—and a foolscap on your silly head."

"Ought to have a look at your own noggin!" Joe appeared to be answering, his tail-end flipping impudently.

At the post-office window in the store, Toivo mailed the box of carvings and received the envelope containing the money order for forty-five dollars, which he showed to the people who owned the store as his father had directed. It was not necessary to impress those good people, Toivo thought, for they ran their business on their trust of others, and everyone along the river could buy from them on credit.

It is just that Father's feeling pretty good today. He grinned to himself. And does like to pay as he goes! Cheerfully then the boy wrote out his long list of supplies. He would cash the money order when he went in to Astoria and pay this bill immediately.

"Salt," he wrote, "sugar, dried prunes, beans, coffee, raisins, coal oil, lamp wicks, matches, cheese, flour." All of these, except the coal oil the store people put into a flour sack so that Toivo could sling it over his shoulder. They gave him a couple of gunnysacks too, to lay across his back and keep the weight of the load from pressing too sharply. The can of coal oil he swung by its bale in his free hand.

For a while he felt almost warm, because the dry sacks kept the air from striking his wet back; but before long he was shivering and wishing that he were home.

"How you doing back there, Funny Face?" he would call now and then to the scrambling young traveler trying to keep up with him; but Joe was too busy and too tired even to give him a sound. Toivo understood how Joe must feel when finally they came back to the float and the young sea lion heaved a big sigh and dropped into a nap. And he understood too how Hadge Jarvenin felt when at sight of the load his son was carrying he sat up in bed and shook both fists in the air as though in congratulation.

"Success, I see!" boomed Hadge's big voice. "The Jarvenins are good customers, eh?"

"Good customers!" Toivo shouted, entering into his

father's spirit of triumph. "Why, in the last hour I have bought out the store—with the good credit the sight of your money order gave us!" One by one and with a flourish he laid all the articles on the table so that they could be admired. "Of course," he added grandly, "these are simply necessities. Wait until tomorrow! Do you know what I am going to buy when I go down to Astoria tomorrow to get the money order cashed?"

"What might that be, young Toivo?" Hadge beamed.

"The biggest piece of stewing beef in Clatsop County!"

"And boots for you, boy. You will get new boots right away, hm?"

"Both of us will get new ones! With the next money order from Jeff Cameron, we'll do that!" Toivo put wood on the fire. He slipped out of his wet clothes and into dry ones and pulled dry wool socks onto his cold feet. "You want to sleep now?" Hadge frowned. "A little while?"

"Only a little while," Hadge agreed.

The next day, leaving his father contented and taking Joe with him, Toivo again went to Astoria. He was to cash the money order from Mr. Cameron.

As on his previous trip, he tied the *Gull* at the foot of Fisher's slip and he and Joe walked up the incline to the street. It was not slippery this time. In the city today hardly a trace of the recent snow could be seen.

"You won't have to walk far, Joe," Toivo assured his seal. "First, we'll go to the post office and get the money. Then we'll pick up all the newspapers we can at the stand and see what they say about you. We can buy the meat on the way back to the boat. This won't take long."

He felt in his purse, to know if Mrs. Ek's safety pin was still there; and it was. He should use the pin, Mrs. Ek had told him, whenever he went to town, carrying money in his shirt pocket. There were shady characters in cities who would steal whatever they could reach. Toivo had never spotted anybody who looked as if he might be one of these people; but it seemed only fair to take the good lady's advice.

Several passers-by on the street smiled at him and at Joe following him, as they had done on the previous trip. One group of boys who seemed to be discussing Joe as they approached nodded and said, "'Lo, Toivo," as they went by; and Toivo nearly halted in his tracks with surprise and pleasure.

"Did you hear that?" he asked in a low voice of Joe. "As though they had known me all their lives. How in blazes—" For a moment he did stand still, relishing a good warm feeling that he had not known before.

It was a pretty fine thing, he thought, to come walking down a street and meet people who said "hello" and called you by name. Made you feel like somebody.

Now you are a well-known man about town, my friend, he said to himself, taking long strides and able to pretend for the length of time it took him to walk the next half block to the post office that he no longer was a "river boy" in threadbare jacket and soggy shoes, but had become a citizen of importance. He turned in at the post-office door.

"Will you please cash this?" he jauntily requested of

the man behind the grilled window, handing him the postal order. Then he let his eyes rove the room.

Wood panels, he noted admiringly. Steam heaters. Pretty fancy! He saw too that a large, well-dressed gentleman stood near one of the windows, reading a newspaper. The man behind the grated window was now asking him something.

"You are Hadge Jarvenin?"

"No, sir. I'm his son." Toivo pointed to his father's signature. "He signed that. Right there."

"That is correct. Do you have identification?"

"Should I?" Toivo felt his sense of importance leave him, knew he must be showing his puzzlement. "Aren't you the boss?"

"I'm the postmaster." The man laughed. "Uncle Sam's my boss."

"Sure."

"You see, I don't know who you are."

"No, you don't." Once more Toivo felt like the unknown river boy.

"You haven't anything with your name on it? Just some thing to show who you are? I've got a strict boss."

"No." How heavy was Toivo's heart! He was not going to take the money home to Hadge. He understood the situation, however.

"Of course—for all you know, I could have found that, hm?"

"Rules." The man looked sorry. "That's the way it is."

"Okay." Toivo took back the money order and put it in his purse. As steadily as he was able, Joe following at his heels, he walked toward the door.

Then, behind him, another voice spoke.

156

FOURTEEN

"I believe," the rich voice behind Toivo was proclaiming, "that this will resolve your dilemma." Over his shoulder he saw that the man who had been reading by the window was addressing him; and that after an authoritative gesture in the direction of the postmaster the man laid his paper on the counter under the postmaster's gaze. That gentleman who had Uncle Sam as his boss glanced at the paper and began to laugh.

"Hold on, Toivo!" he called. "I know you now!" Toivo spun around. He saw a picture of himself looking up from the counter—the picture of him that Jeff Cameron had taken as he tossed a fish for Joe. And there was a caption: "Breakfast for Joe Whiskers, Hero of the Lower Columbia."

"Hello, Toivo," said the postmaster with a smile, sliding his window grating to put out a hand and shake with the boy, then leaning out over his counter for a better look at his other customer. "Howdy, hero!"

"*Awr,*" returned Joe.

"How will you have your money, Toivo?" The postmaster took four ten-dollar bills and a five from the cash drawer. "This all right? Want them in an envelope?"

"Four of those in an envelope, please." Relief began

to flow through Toivo. "And the little one for the purse." He received the bill for the purse, shoved this down into his pants pocket, but with the envelope of money to be pinned inside his shirt pocket he had some difficulty. He was not much used to safety pins.

"Permit me," offered the big man who had found his picture in the paper. "I'm an old hand at that." He had shrewd but friendly eyes. It took him only a moment to pin the money into the shirt pocket, and Toivo buttoned his jacket tight over the bulge of it. Then he wanted to leave. He was suddenly in a hurry to get hold of all the papers at the newsstand and to find out what they had to say about Joe.

"Thanks," he said with a quick nod of good-by to both men, and turned toward the street; but the big man walked along with him.

"Young Toivo Jarvenin," he said, his black mustache lifting to show a flash of white teeth as he smiled, his eyes probing, "I enjoyed reading about you. A boy who wants to be a doctor should be in school, my friend."

"Yes. I know." Toivo, in full agreement, looked up at him.

"Well?"

"We—live upriver, almost to Svenson. Too far." (That was enough of a reason for a stranger. You didn't explain to everyone you met that at the present time you had neither the clothes to wear to high school nor the money to buy books.)

"That—is the reason?"

"It's a long way, really."

"Some people won't stop at anything. Heard of a

158

fellow once who had to walk a long way—to borrow books. Name of Abe Lincoln."

"I read about it." Toivo looked up, puzzled. "But what does he have to—"

"He has to do with all men," replied the one with the fine, deep voice, "especially those who want to learn. You read a good deal, young Toivo?"

"Yes, sir. Everything I can get." Toivo began to realize that this was no ordinary conversation or an ordinary man; and he felt the shrewd eyes, speculating.

"If the first year high-school texts were available, should you—ah—care to peruse them?"

"Oh, yes!" The light in Toivo's face must have been convincing; for the big man laughed aloud.

"In approximately three days, then—begin perusing!"

"Are you the—school superintendent?"

"Correct."

"Wow." Toivo stood very still and tried to believe that this was happening to him. "I can't tell you— how many times—I've wished for a chance like this!"

"Wished?" His companion chuckled. "You may have heard the wishing story I like to tell when I'm visiting schools."

"I haven't heard that."

"It concerns two children who were still a long way from school one morning when across the fields they heard the warning bell ring; and both of them, unwilling to face a strict teacher, wished hard that they were safely seated at their desks. 'Let's get down on our knees,' one child said, 'and pray that we'll make it on time.' But the other child took a grip on her lunchbox and lengthened her stride. 'I'm prayin', all right,' she replied, 'but I'm hikin' while I pray!'"

Toivo chuckled. Then quickly he said good-by, for, with a bow of farewell, his new friend was turning down another street. As things came about, Toivo never saw the school man again, but he was to hear from him.

"Come on, Joe," he now urged the tiring young sea lion. Only two more places for us to go, the newsstand and the butcher shop. In a few minutes you will have a good rest in the boat." He began to wish he had brought with him the two apples he'd left in the *Gull*. It was getting on to noontime and the eating places in a city like this always seemed to send out extra-good food smells at this hour. He bought the local news and three out-of-town papers at the newsstand; then, with the four of these pushed under his arm, hustled Joe away from the place. The news vendor's helper and some bystanders had recognized the sea lion from the news stories and unfeelingly crowded him. Joe had resented it. When some of the men pushed him with their boots, his gentle eyes had turned hard. He had drawn back his lips, threatened with his sharp teeth, and given Toivo a scare. If Joe had bitten somebody—

"You're all tired out," he soothed, moving toward the butcher shop. "And, sure—disappointed in people. You have to find out sometime, though. There are that kind. Come on, shake a flipper. One more stop to make."

They found no other customers in the butcher shop and apparently the proprietor here had not seen the papers. He showed little curiosity about Joe. Toivo was able to make a careful selection of the meat he had promised his father.

"A good customer," the butcher told him. "There should be a weiner for you." He slid back the glass panel of his counter. "A weiner for you—a fish for your seal." He handed the weiner, tossed the fish. And Joe, of course, with a wiggle and a snatch neatly caught his gift. Boy and seal then, blissfully licking their lips, ambled down the incline of the slip and climbed into their boat to start home.

"So far," mumbled Toivo through a mouthful of juicy apple as he cast off, "not such a bad trip." But Joe looked back at him with sparks in his eyes.

"*Aw-hoowr?* [Which part of it?]" asked Joe. Toivo gave him another piece of fish, this time from the boat's fish box, and he became his usual cheerful self, settling into a nap as they moved upstream.

"Once we get past the Point," decided Toivo, "I'm just going to let the old *Gull* idle a bit, and grab a look at those headlines." He was finding it difficult to wait longer to know what Jeff Cameron had written.

"You should have known better! Never take your hands from the steering!" he fumed at himself a few minutes afterward. "Never throttle down in a bad current!" He did know better. Hadn't he been warned all his life? And heard others told?

"In winter," any river man would have said, "when you're bucking the current in a small boat—keep her gunned!" Toivo now learned this maxim again from experience. He felt his small craft sweep out of control and roll broadside to the current.

He got his hands back to the tiller. You didn't panic when you had made a mistake like this. He'd been taught that maxim too. You took hold, and you held. In a wide, easy circle you brought your boat about, not choking or stalling your engine—not forcing too much—just easing over, and back on course.

He drew a long, unsteady breath. The bad minutes were over; and he headed the *Gull* for home.

"Well, all right!" he snapped at Joe, who was awake and watching closely. "So I did turn out to be a bum navigator! Go back to sleep!"

The sea lion's nap continued even after he and Toivo reached home. Toivo put away the package of meat, turned around, waving his newspapers; and Mrs. Ek, who had been holding the cards for two hands while she and her husband played a four-hand game with Hadge, pushed the cards aside and patted a place on the bed cover. Toivo noticed they had brought up the mail and that his father had a letter from Hameenlinna lying beside him among others, but in the excitement of the moment and the press of circumstances later on, Toivo neglected to ask about this mail.

"Toivo," cried Mrs. Ek, "put those papers right here!"

"And read them aloud!" added Mr. Ek. Toivo laid the papers on the bed but shook his head in regard to the rest of the order.

"Somebody else do it, please," he said. "I'm starving!" In no time at all he was deep in a cup of coffee and working his way through a sandwich. Mrs. Ek began slowly to read aloud the captions under different pictures in the papers.

" 'Breakfast for Joe Whiskers, Hero of the Lower Columbia,' " it says here. " ' Father and Son Owe Lives to Pet Sea Lion. Have You Seen Any Sea Lion Gentlemen,

Lately?' and 'Doughty Old Man-of-the-Sea Arrives in Time.'" Mrs. Ek's eyes were full of stars when she looked up, her face pink as a peony.

"Why, we'll all be marked characters!" she exclaimed. "Everybody who comes from this place. Your ocean lion, Toivo—he'll make us famous!"

"Wait until you hear this." Toivo had finished his lunch and now sat down to take over the reading. He sent a wink in his father's direction before starting, knowing that Hadge would have difficulty in enduring journalistic verbiage. "Listen—

"'You have not heard until today the name of Hadge Jarvenin, artist-craftsman, because he comes from another land; nor do you know of Toivo, his son, who hopes to be a doctor. Thanks to their pet sea lion, Joe, however, who rescued the two of them on Christmas morning from the ice-cold depths of the Columbia River, you are likely to hear of both of these people in the future, and to learn of the gifts for America they hold in their hands.'" At this point Toivo chuckled. Hadge had pretended to groan—loudly—in protest.

"Won't hurt you!" declared Mrs. Ek. "Not a mite!"

"'Meanwhile,'" Toivo read on, "'Joe the sea lion enjoys to the fullest his role as leading character in this unusual drama and continues to devour quantities of fish brought to him by admirers. He guards the houseboat on which he makes his home with the Jarvenins, and grows at amazing speed. In truth it is Joe's rate of increase in size and weight, plus the hazard presented in his area by an army of seal hunters, which makes a future for Joe the sea lion, vastly improbable.'" Toivo hesitated on the last words, but completed the reading.

There was more along the same lines in the other papers. All the reports told of Joe's rescue of the brave Toivo and the talented Hadge, mentioning somewhere in the story Hadge's despair while wasting his years on a fish scow, and Toivo's thwarted hope of an education. Jeff Cameron had known exactly what he was doing when he wrote "Joe's story." (And Doctor Smith knew too how the newsman was going to handle it. That's why he looked so pleased about it, Toivo thought.)

Well, he did it all for us, the three of us. He put the papers away and walked thoughtfully to look out the window. The stories were for the most part lightly worded, sometimes humorous; but they managed to carry to a reader a feeling of life on the river and something of the wonder that was Joe. Toivo guessed that they were the kind of stories Mr. Cameron had promised they would be.

"You don't—object to the write-ups, Father?" he asked; and the sick man, with unusual cheer, shook his head. (Toivo was to recall later that he had wondered about the reason for Hadge's good spirits, and then to better understand them.)

"No harm done," Hadge had replied. "Not unless my Cousin Joe objects to being called a hero."

"And that," laughed the Eks, getting ready to return home, "Joe does not."

Other papers carrying the stories about Joe and the family on the houseboat came from various places in the United States during the next ten days as the original articles were recopied. After that—a deluge of letters. Letters and a stream of gift packages came flowing through the country post office to the houseboat on the Columbia.

"You must not give up, Mr. Jarvenin," the letters told Hadge. "Hold on a little longer. Something will come up for you." "Know that we think of you and wish you well," many of the letters said. "We too have known trouble." Some of the messages carried praise for Toivo. "Your country will be proud of you," they told him.

"People send presents!" the awed Toivo reported to Aarni. "Cookies—and jam. Ladies knit things for us!"

"More power to 'em." Aarni approved of all this.

"One man made a proposition. Said he would build a tank or a pool. We could put Joe in it, and charge admission for people to see him do his tricks. The man didn't seem to know that a sea lion is happy only in cold fresh water—and that it should be sea water."

"Didn't know, didn't care." Aarni scowled. "Going to answer that one?"

"Maybe he—meant well."

"Ha!" snorted Aarni.

Hadge's pale face began to take on color as the days moved along with their offerings of friendship from previously unknown men and women. Old warmth came into his eyes.

"Like neighbors!" he would exclaim as he opened mail. "The same as at home." He asked that each "neighbor" be sent a note of thanks, and left that responsibility to Toivo, as he now left many other responsibilities.

In fact, the boy reflected, his father appeared to have a whole new slant on life since his accident. But what kind of change was this? It had been a long time since Hadge ordered his son to come or to go, to do this or to do that, or since he had made any kind of plans at all. Surely this was not good! Had big Hadge Jarvenin, the artist, lost his dream for the future, become so tame that he would carve figurines forever for bread-and-butter money, content to leave well enough alone? Or was it possible—that there might be another reason to account for his lack of concern? (There seemed no time any more to sit down and talk things over, Toivo thought.)

"Why do you suppose," Toivo asked Aarni the next time he saw him, "that my father is willing to drift along the way he is doing? He never says a word about his wanting to go to Finland. And he knows I'm on the spot and have to do something about Joe, but he never mentions him any more either."

"Could be your pa's played out, the way a good fightin' salmon gets, and is doing the way the salmon does, restin' up for another try. Maybe he figures, well, he's earnin' enough with his carving to let him rest for a while." Aarni considered his own words for a moment, shook his head. "Don't seem like him, though. Always before, he's been roarin' around that he wanted to get away from here, somewhere so you could go to school."

"Yes. I'm going to have to ask him, point blank, what's wrong." Toivo paced restlessly, then came to the most pressing of his problems. "Aarni, Joe is getting awfully big."

"Sure is."

"He shakes the float when he climbs onto it. Another

166

little while, and he could tip us. He's a big, easy target, too."

"I know."

"Soon—he will be in danger again—when the salmon run starts."

"Yep. Yep, he will."

January, a long, gray month, went by with Hadge sitting in his chair, steadily carving. And his skill grew as he carved the funny, wise, sad, and wistful little wooden people Jeff Cameron sold for him across the country. They were bringing higher prices now, as the young man had predicted; and Toivo could see his father's satisfaction in paying bills and providing for the needs of his son and himself. How could anyone find the heart to remind this apparently peaceful man just recovering from an accident that his security was a temporary thing? That the "nest egg for the future" Hadge always had planned was nowhere in sight?

February and March went by. Toivo worked for Mr. Ek on his five days, and, as the school man had said, "perused" his studies at night. And often he longed for help with both tasks. Joe was so fond of fishing and of eating that it took hours from both farm and schoolwork to stand guard over him.

Pussy willows came out along the river bank, daffodils bloomed in the yards; and April arrived in soft, warm rain, a blur of green and growing things. Spring gardening started at the Ek farm, and there were little calves to feed. If only he could have settled down to any one of these jobs, Toivo felt that he might have done well with it; but now he was not showing good results on any score.

"Those school grades have to be kept up," he told Aarni. "What I do in high school will follow me into pre-med. And you know how much I want to do things right for Mr. Ek. When Joe is in sight, all is well. The minute he disappears I'm sure something has gone wrong for him." Aarni's blue eyes looked into those of his friend. He said something under his breath: "What will be, will be—*Mikä on, se on.*"

"Aarn!"

"You know that's what the old-country people say."

"And what"—Toivo looked back at him—"does Aarni Rekkonen say?"

"He says—" The tall boy's eyes began to dance. "That crazy guy says—that if you want a thing to turn a certain way, by gar you've got to give it a nudge in that direction!"

"That's what I thought," nodded Toivo.

One night, tired in body and mind from a long day of extra work in the garden and an evening of schoolwork followed by a tedious search for Joe before that young fellow could be safely bedded down, Toivo once more lay under his covers and searched for the answers he needed. Hadge was already sleeping, as though he had not a worry in the world.

I've watched him a couple of times lately, though, Toivo said to himself. He sits sometimes and—strokes Joe's head. Once again he wondered if his father could be as truly unconcerned as he had appeared to be in the months just passed.

168

For me, going on and on like this, waiting for the worst to happen, is as stupid as holding still to let a rock fall on my head. Only—in this case the rock is aimed at Joe. Every hour of every day I have him on my mind, knowing that sooner or later trouble will strike.

Toivo heard a scratching at the window then and saw the wishful whiskered face of the sea lion against the glass as the young animal took a last look for the night. In the code they always had between them, tip of third finger and tip of thumb touching and arm raised, he gave him the "all's-well" signal.

At once the sad look slid from the sea pup's face. Joe's big eyes twinkled, and he made a silly motion with his head. Then his weight shook the floor as he flipped onto his back, once more hunkered down to sleep.

Toivo tossed and turned. Pictures of Joe as he had known him went clicking through his mind: the day he'd found the helpless pup; the first time the scared youngster had jumped from the dock; the morning he had stood up to Bingo and won a place for himself at the milking; the night he had stolen the fish and begun to grow out of babyhood; and Christmas Eve, when he had come home again from banishment at sea. He thought of the night when Joe had been shot by a hunter and come creeping home for help; and he remembered the shiny barrel of the revolver on the drug-store counter.

Is that what is to be, little Joe Whiskers? A hunter's bullet for you—and shadows somewhere? Or a quick ending at Father's hand? Am I—going to say yes to one of these?

Think of something! his heart cried. His tired young

body sank into sleep while yet his thoughts prodded him: Make a move—some kind of a move to save Joe. *There's no more time.*

The room was gray with daylight when he awoke. Hadge still slept. Mr. Ek would be getting up about now. The phrase "make a move" must have stayed all night in his mind, he thought, for there it was as soon as he was conscious this morning. It brought back Aarni's words too: A fellow who wants a thing to happen . . . has to give a nudge in that direction. This was the way Doctor Smith too would have talked. He had told stories of how he had got his education under difficulties. *Doctor Smith.* Hey!

Toivo threw back his covers, sat straight up in bed, and for a moment considered the idea that had come to him. Why hadn't he thought of this sooner!

With quick, decisive motions he pulled on his clothes. Toivo Jarvenin was about to "give a nudge."

FIFTEEN

He was thankful to be able to tiptoe out of the house without awakening his father and hoped also to make it across the runway while Joe slept. That young lolloper, however, was close behind him before he had gone halfway.

I wasn't trying to sneak away from you, Toivo assured the happy young animal in his thoughts, waiting briefly for him to rock alongside. It was just that I didn't want you to hear me, Joe, when I try to get rid of you.

The Eks were finishing breakfast when he walked into their kitchen and asked to use the telephone; but soon they went outside, one to his barn chores and the other to feed her chickens. Joe had waited on the porch. Toivo had the house to himself when he cranked for central and put in his call.

"Tillamook, please," he said to the operator, remembering to hold his voice down and pleased to hear it sounding on a firm business level. "Doctor Smith's home."

He had a good connection; the doctor's words came clearly over the wire.

"Everything all right, Toivo?"

"Nobody is sick."

"Glad to hear that." There was a moment of silence. "Do anything for you?"

"For—Joe and me."

"Nothing's happened to him!"

"Not—yet." Toivo swallowed.

"Come on, boy."

"Well, I was thinking, one time—the time when we put him out over the bar and I was stewing around about what might happen to him—you said something I have just now remembered."

"Hmm."

"Maybe you were only trying to make me feel better, but you said that Joe might head for a place you'd heard of, where sea lions live."

"That's Three Arch Rocks at Oceanside. It did seem one hope for him at the time. He didn't do it though, of course."

"That time he came home. But now—"

"Now Joe again? The salmon run will soon be on full tilt, won't it?"

"There will be an army of seal hunters." Toivo took a long breath and continued, his voice still level. "What I wanted was to ask you—*how about those rocks now?*"

"To tell the truth, I've never been there." The doctor's concern was in his quick reply. "I'll certainly find out something about the place right away. You sound like calamity."

"Well, there's some shooting all the time, and Joe won't—stay home as well as he used to." In spite of all he could do, Toivo's voice wobbled.

172

"Hold it." The doctor spoke quickly. "Let me get my wits together." He was thinking hard.

"You are awfully busy. I guess I shouldn't—"

"Tell you what. This Sunday I'm going to be driving in the direction of the coast on business. I'll go on over to Oceanside and try to bring back some information for you."

"If you say that it is okay for Joe to be put over there, Doctor—I'd do it."

"I'm grateful for your confidence. It raises my self-esteem at least two notches. Now we'll find out if that up trend is justified, eh? Can you and Joe hold on over there a little longer?"

"Try."

"I'll drop you a line—the minute I get back."

Now that I have been over there to the Rocks [reported the doctor's note when it came], I'm dumfounded that I have previously heard so little about the place. It is beautiful. Has been a government-owned refuge for wild life since 1907, when the then President Theodore Roosevelt set the area aside.

A friend took me out and around the Rocks in his small boat, and we saw some of the interesting inhabitants. Snaky-necked, green-eyed birds called cormorants fly all over the place. They are black. Funny, awkward birds called puffins sit or waddle on the ledges as if weighted down by their prow-shaped beaks. Thousands of other birds are there. And there is a herd of sea lions who make this their permanent home. Probably two hundred of them. Of course, for you and Joe Whiskers, my questions were about these.

It is breeding and birthing season in the herd right now, the people who live nearby tell me; and for this reason we did not venture too close. The roaring of those big bull sea lions fighting to hold their own families together is a fierce and warning sound. That roaring can be heard far back in the hills, after one has left the beach.

The old-timers told me, too, that often baby sea lions (like Joe was when you first saw him), are seen playing or resting on the sands opposite Three Arch Rocks. There are laws against moving them. Their mothers come after them when it is time for them to return home, and nudge them back again through the waves.

I learned many things, Toivo. And I don't want you too disappointed when I tell you that in spite of that, I am no closer now to stating that this is the place for Joe than I was on the day we last talked by phone. I simply do not know. Nobody else whom I questioned, either, was willing to hazard a guess as to what might happen if a young male sea lion were suddenly dumped uninvited on the doorstep of an established colony like this.

I wanted very much to bring you good news, and hope, my friend. You will understand that it is difficult for me to do otherwise.

A suggestion does cross my mind, however. Will you be in the Eks' kitchen at noon on Thursday? I'll call you by phone.

Your friend, Eb Smith.

Thursday. It seemed a long way off. So many hours until then, in which Joe could meet trouble. At last, however, the day did come. The noon hour came; and Toivo waited for the doctor's call. Mrs. Ek was preparing dinner, Mr. Ek finishing some morning work, Joe biding his time out on the porch with his face against Mrs. Ek's clean window and his big eyes looking in, and Hadge, when last Toivo saw him, had been busy with his carving. When the bell rang, Toivo was instantly there.

"Hello. HELLO."

"Well, I've a proposition for you," came Doctor Smith's voice. "You may think it's wild."

"Bet I don't."

"I have been checking my camping equipment. I have a fairly good tent, two cots that will hold up, and a decent little stove. How would you like to borrow them?"

"I—guess you're joking."

"No. Seriously. I'll tell you, Toivo, I've been thinking for some time that a change of location would be good for Hadge. For you too, so far as that goes. My suggestion is this: that you and your father—*and Joe*—spend a couple of restful months over there at Oceanside. You can fish and read and loaf, and Hadge can carve. And while the two of you build up health and stamina for whatever this winter is to bring to you—who knows? It is just possible that Mr. Joe Whiskers may cooperate. He may help find a few answers for himself and his problem."

"Blazes! Doctor!"

"Mind you, this may not work. We have no assurance that the experiment will be successful for Joe. He may always be unfriendly to his own kind, now, or they may never accept him. We can't count on a thing; and you must guard against doing so. We would be finding out, though, what his chances are, perhaps. And at the same time—be giving him as much protection as possible if he needed friends."

"Yes! Oh it sounds—" Toivo's eager acceptance cut itself off. "No, it wouldn't work," he said dispiritedly, his voice dragging. "My father never would agree to it."

"*Mitä täälä tapahtun?*—[What goes on here?]"
"*What is this?*"

The voice was Hadge's. He had unexpectedly followed his son, to learn what this call was about. In a fury, Toivo whirled on him!

"What *is* this? *It's a chance!* For Joe! But he'll never get it! Because you are going to run off to your Suomi the minute you're able—" Hot tears stung his eyes and he angrily shook them away. "And we can't give it to him!"

Very slowly Hadge took the receiver into his own hand. One emotion or feeling seemed to flood the big man and with unusual clarity to stamp itself on his face. That feeling was amazement. He put the receiver to his ear and spoke into the mouthpiece.

"Doctor, will you please repeat to me exactly what you have just said to Toivo?" He listened. It seemed to Toivo that he listened for long minutes.

"But I explained," he said at last, "that I no longer planned to go. No more thought of returning to the old country." ("I—no more!") These were the words, so long untranslated, which Hadge had murmured as he regained consciousness. Toivo's heart began to pound.

176

"I did *not* explain it?" Hadge shook his head, grew red in the face, and appeared ready to explode. "How can that be! All this time—all this time—I have thought everyone knew I would never trouble my son so greatly again!" He quieted, again listened.

"Yes. Of course, I understand. After such a blow on the head, one does for a while confuse things." (Instead of his drifting along all this time, thought Toivo, excitement running through him, instead of his giving up, he has been planning a new life, right here in America!)

"I am expecting my brother here in the fall," Hadge was continuing. "Yes, in business together. In Portland. Good opportunity for Toivo. I am sure you will understand, Doctor Smith, though my son does not, that he and his happiness are my only real ambition. His sealion pet is part of his happiness. Therefore— Thank you; we shall gladly accept your offer."

Hadge turned from the telephone, and stepped into the biggest bear hug Toivo's strong young arms could deliver!

This decision to go to the beach for the summer had been a swift one, and swift action must follow to get everything taken care of and ready for the leavetaking. Hadge, Toivo, and Joe left the houseboat on the Columbia for their camp at the sea coast within a few days after Toivo's call from his friend Doctor Smith. For once Hadge's thoughts were dealing more with the future than were his son's. Toivo found it hard to leave. His good friends were here, his home, the garden and the farm animals. Good-bys were not easy to face.

The Eks and the Rekkonens went down to the dock

to wave them off on the *Sue Elmore;* and Aarni, as deck hand, helped with everything. He would be with them also, Toivo reminded himself, when it came time to unload on the dock at Tillamook. He would be a big help with Joe.

The young sea lion was not in a crate this time. He rocked up the slip and across the loading dock under his own power, and though he pushed nervously close to Toivo's legs, his bright glance went everywhere.

"I'm glad I was here long enough to help get the garden in," Toivo told the Eks. "I'll be thinking of it all summer over there. All the rest of the year too."

"When we come to visit you," they promised, "we shall bring some of your vegetables."

"Tomatoes?"

"Ehka—[Possibly]." Little Mr. Ek and Big Mrs. Ek smiled at one another, remembering, Toivo knew, how fond of those juicy fruits he their hired man always had been, and no doubt recalling the dirty face he must have presented most of the time, from devouring a large share of the crop.

Yes, he felt glad that he could leave the garden flourishing. And he was well satisfied with arrangements he had made for his school tests. They could be taken just as well in another county, the Astoria office had notified him when he had written of his move. And "I know you will do well" the superintendent had written in pencil along the edge of the letter form.

He was glad too that Hadge had made a gift of the motorboat *Gull* to Mr. and Mrs. Ek in gratitude for all they had done for him; and that he, Toivo, had given his skiff to Olli and Selina. But his heart grieved because there was nothing for Aarni. No parting gift for Aarni, best friend of all.

When they had waved their last good-by, and when the *Sue Elmore* had made her run to Tillamook and they were on the dock there, checking their belongings while Doctor Smith and Joe waited nearby in a light wagon the doctor had borrowed, Toivo tried to find words to tell Aarni how he felt.

"I just don't have any way of showing my thanks," he told him. "I wish I could—"

Aarni's direct blue gaze cut him short. "No need, Toiv. Between us, no need for proof. Huh?"

"But I am—awfully obliged to you."

"Me too! To you!" Aarni's face, which had grown red with embarrassment, suddenly crinkled in laughter. "I sound like a train! Here!" He shoved Toivo toward the wagon, where Hadge already had found his seat, and boosted him into the wagon bed topsy-turvy beside Joe. "All aboard!"

The horses started off at a trot. Toivo sat up and looked back. Aarni was standing there in the middle of the road, not smiling now, his gaze following the wagon. In a few minutes the tall boy, the *Sue Elmore* and the harbor, and the little city were left behind. Along the rutted seven-mile road to the beach the wagon jolted its way. Toivo's hand stroked Joe's round head; his own head lay for a moment against the long, supple neck.

Would this strange young sea animal with his love and understanding of the ways of men go back to the life of his own kind, the boy wondered? Would Joe try to make friends with those fierce old bulls who ruled this part of the ocean? Or would they fight him? Send him to his fate—this awful way?

As the doctor said, no one knew. They were taking a chance—Joe's only chance.

"Come on now, boy," he whispered to the young seal, seeing how anxious he looked. "Don't worry."

Joe did worry, though. As he started in the jolting wagon down that dusty road it was as if he shared the same feeling that weighed on Toivo, as if he knew that somehow time had caught up with him and with all of them, and that soon now this strange road would lead them apart, one from the other.

When they made camp that night on the beach opposite Three Arch Rocks, the young animal crept close to Toivo, his whiskered face turned toward the sea, his great eyes sad.

Toivo remembered afterward that he had reached an arm to him, but that he had not been able to stay awake long enough to talk with him. The wash of the surf, the monotonous distant voices of the sea lions on the Rocks, and his own fatigue, had put him quickly to sleep.

SIXTEEN

As the gray gulls flew, easily and without haste, so the sunny days winged by at Oceanside for Toivo and Joe. The young seal gave no trouble, but lent a happiness of his own and a seeming awareness of their closeness in comradeship during this interlude, which the boy knew would remain always in his own memory.

There seemed no immediate need for hurry. At first it was not disturbing that Joe ignored the existence close by of creatures like himself and that he steadfastly denied any interest in them. Even after two weeks of surf splashing near shore, his refusal to venture out past the breakers unless Toivo went with him seemed overly cautious but not alarming insofar as successfully carrying out the plans for him was concerned.

This suspicious—perhaps even fearful—Joe Whiskers had after all twice been deserted at sea in his short life; but surely after a while he would grow curious about the other animals, the ones on the Rocks. It seemed reasonable to expect, Toivo told himself, that he would at least one day want to make himself known to them.

"Best to give him all the time he wants, don't you think?" Toivo asked his father. And Hadge, smoking a pipe contentedly, nodded agreement.

"I think it will not take too long," he said. "I have watched him—listening."

"You noticed that? He does it often. Tips his head, gets that faraway look in his eyes, as if he's listening to some sound beyond our hearing."

"Who is to say wild things do not?"

With Joe close by, Toivo swam and fished, hunted in the warm salt-water pools for shells and small sea creatures left by the tides, or made an occasional trip to the store or post office. With Joe steadfastly gazing in the other direction he stood on his lookout point above the camp and studied through his binoculars the sea lions out on the Rocks. In resting or in restless moods, those creatures so like his own pet and yet so different from him, were fascinating.

The mating season, with its constant fighting between bull seals, began to draw to a close, and the roaring from the rocky ledges toned down to a calmer sound. Now the animals rested, took to a life of casual fishing and diving, with long snoozes in the sunshine, and—in the case of the mothers—to the nursing of the new young.

Several times Toivo came upon one of the small nursing pups as it rested on the sandy shore. And it looked so much like the helpless young Joe he once had rescued that he had to remind himself sternly that he was not needed here, in fact was not permitted to lend a hand (unless there was proof the pup had been orphaned) because then the pup's mother might be too disturbed to return for him.

A few times he glimpsed little "gangs" of last year's pups, Joe's age and about his size, but seemingly less able to look out for themselves. In fact they appeared to him bewildered and uncertain in manner, and to have clubbed together for companionship.

Poor little guys, he said to them in his thoughts, watching through the glasses. Your moms sort of pushed you out the door, didn't they, to make room for your new brothers and sisters. Look, you can take it, all right. Come on and shake a flipper out there. *Now* you grow up!

One day he reached for Joe, put a hand on either side of that young mariner's head, and turned it in the direction of the other pups.

"Look away out there—that splashing. Know what that is? Your object lesson, that's what! You have got to grow up too, Joe." Toivo had begun to feel he should do a little urging. "Those other sea pups are little Mister Whiskerses too, Joe. They like to play some of the same games you play. So—why can't you just give a glance their way?"

"Aw-hoowr!" scoffed Joe, pulling back, looking down his nose. "What do I have in common with that wild lot?"

When August arrived and one day Toivo realized that only four weeks were left of this try to find a life for Joe, and that apparently no progress at all had been made in that direction his hopes faltered.

That night he lay awake for a long time. It was high tide and the surf boomed close by. Moonlight lay in a golden path across the water from shore to the sea-lion refuge as though to beckon any lost or lonely ones who wished to come. Toivo sat up, looked out the tent opening. The light softened the outlines of the great Rocks, lending them even more beauty than they held by day. The sea lions' roaring was muted by the wash of the surf; and all the scene was one of peace.

If I should see old Joe headed out there now, he thought, if I knew he'd stay—and even if I knew I'd never see him again—I think I could take it. But Joe was not walking any golden path to a new life that night. That young walloper slept snugly in the tent, close to Toivo's bed.

"Are you going to wait too long, Joe? Has all this been for nothing?" The old ache returned to his heart, the worry to his thoughts.

At about that time a thing happened that no one had foreseen or planned. One of the sea pups left the others out at the Rocks and came inshore to look around; and Joe came face to face with it! Toivo, who had been standing waist deep in the surf and watching Joe perform one of his fast runs in circles, saw it happen. He had not realized any more than had Joe that the other young seal was near, until the two whiskered faces zoomed toward one another, then stopped nose to nose in popeyed surprise. Then Toivo was as startled as anyone.

"Easy, ea-sy," he whispered to himself and to Joe. "Don't spoil it." He hardly dared move, hoped against hope that all would be well, and held his breath as long as he could, then exhaled carefully as the two youngsters, after staring one another in the face, suddenly dived—and dived again—and again—as if to show off.

"That is what they are doing too." Toivo grinned,

moving at last to the beach and to the door of his own tent, where he could sit and watch this story unfold itself. All the next week he sat there or walked on the sand, watching through his binoculars. The young ones played every day, sometimes in the morning, sometimes in the afternoon. They both returned home at night.

Once his amazement had worn off, Joe appeared to take that other pup into his care and to be trying to make a man of the world of him. If the poor ignoramus didn't learn fast, what of that? He could at least see how it was done. Joe made his playmate try over and over again the Joe Whiskers method of doing the backward flip, the reverse at high speed while going in circles that he had perfected in the Columbia, and the trick of tossing sea kelp high in the air and catching it on his nose as he had caught Selina's ball.

"If we had the gramophone with us, I wonder if he'd—" Toivo started once to say to his father; but Hadge's mind was on his carving.

Gradually Joe and his new friend moved farther out into the surf to play their games, and sometimes now other young sea lions would join them. But during this time Joe always came home to sleep, curling tiredly in his place beside Toivo's bed and expecting in the morning to have his breakfast tossed to him. This too changed.

There came a night when only Hadge and Toivo sat beside the driftwood fire on the beach. Toivo watched the surface of the water as long as there was any light at all. No bobbing round head was visible. There appeared to be no unusual disturbance out at the Rocks; though the reports of the fierce old bull sea lions out there haunted him. He kept the bonfire blazing all night after Hadge was asleep, in case Joe might have lost his bearings in the ocean someplace and needed a beacon to get home. When the dawn came, cold with rolling mists, he crept to bed to rest; but his thoughts hurt him.

Where did you sleep, Joe? He felt empty, deserted, like the spot there beside him where he was used to seeing a funny tan body and a funny whiskered face. You all right—somewhere?

"Aw-whoor! [Just great!]" replied Joe's cheerful voice at the doorway; and there the silly clown was, telling the world how happy he felt to find his family still here— telling Toivo he'd like his breakfast, please, *now,* because he had a date!

Joe came and went after that at irregular intervals. A night at home, two nights away. Now at the end of August, the end of summer and vacation and of the try to help Joe, Toivo had not seen the little clown for ten days and nights. Tomorrow they'd be leaving for Portland.

There had been mist along the coast and about Three Arch Rocks. Fall was in the air, but the afternoons were golden. The sea lions on the Rocks were more quiet than they had been earlier in the season, spent more time sleeping in the sun. But whether Joe was with them or not, Toivo's glasses could not tell him.

If he isn't there, where is he? Where would he go? And if he is that close, why doesn't he come to see me?

This was the day of leaving. Camp had been struck. Tent, stove, cots—all were neatly piled, ready to be picked up and put into the wagon when Doctor Smith should come with it.

I'm going away now, Joe. Toivo's thoughts kept reaching out to his missing pet in spite of all he could do to keep himself busy and try not to act childish. Where are you, Joe? You okay?

His father's hand finally rumpled his hair. "From the high point you might get a look. *Noh?* [Yes?]"

"I've looked my eyes out."

"The doctor will not mind waiting a few minutes."

"All I ask is one little glimpse—to know he's all right."

"Run up there."

Lightly, breaking scarcely a twig of the kinnikinnick and salal growth underfoot, Toivo leaped up the incline to the place he and Joe had known, pulling his binoculars from their case as he climbed.

Except for the creaking cry of gulls overhead as the gray birds wheeled in the sky, and the tiny splash of surf below and the muted hollow roar of the sea lion herd on the Rocks, no sound disturbed this quiet morning.

Would he be in luck this time? Toivo stood on his lookout, searched, searched through his binoculars. Could he, after all, expect to see the one animal out there who was different from the others because of his light color and the streak down his side, his funny face and expressive eyes—who used to think he belonged with people?

You did belong with us too. If it hadn't been for you, Joe, most of the good things that had happened to us would never have come. You were our good luck.

187

He rested a few minutes, again long and earnestly searched the Rocks and the surf.

"So much—you remembered so much, Joe. Have you —forgotten me?"

Hope dimmed at last.

He should have known better, he told himself, than to expect— Of course he never would see old Joe again. Not quite steadily he lowered the binoculars and turned away—but something caught his eye. Something—a weathered piling just off shore? A tan figure, motionless in the shallows! Quickly he peered through the glass again!

The tawny shape was a sea lion. He was lighter in color than any of the others, and down his side where once a bullet had plowed a furrow was the streak of white hair Toivo knew! The young fellow's face was toward shore. Steadily, his great eyes gazed.

How far can he see? Is he looking up here at me? He seems to be!

Involuntarily the boy raised his arm. With the tip of thumb and tip of third finger touching in the code he and Joe had known between them, he gave the all's-well signal; and across his face his old grin flashed. He had an answer!

With undiminished impudence, Joe had done his backward flip!

For a moment, from far away, it was as if there came again that breath of secret laughter.

Toivo's sea-blue eyes held the peace of the scene around him. He went down the hill and on his way.

EPILOGUE

Travelers up and down the Oregon seacoast hear a legend that persists year after year. It concerns a light-colored—sometimes spoken of as "white"—sea lion, seen here, seen there. A young bull, they say it is, already giant size. He is said to play now and then just outside the breakers; has been known to come ashore, as though looking for something.

Old-timers repeat this story to newcomers. Guides on horseback rides and fishing trips charm their clients with the legend.

ABOUT THE AUTHOR

MARGARET ADAIR was born in Portland, Oregon. She started her literary career at the age of seven with speeches from an apple box to her friends on such subjects as "You Should Always Feed Animals and Be Kind to Them Even if They Are a Skunk." She attended Oregon State University and was graduated from San Jose State College of Education, California. After taking time out to serve as an Army nurse, she taught school, acted as city playground instructor, and coached children's puppet and theater groups. She and her husband now live in Sherwood, Oregon, where A FAR VOICE CALLING was planned and partly "set down" in the kitchen of the big old house they bought and undertook to remodel. Readings and criticism from her sons helped shape the story. Mrs. Adair has been contributor to a number of magazines and newspapers; this is her first novel for young readers.

G52